Murder on Highway 2

A Claire Burke Mystery
(Book 5)

by

Emma Pivato

For information, email Cozy Cat Press, cozycatpress@aol.com or visit our website at: www.cozycatpress.com

COZY CAT
PRESS

ISBN: 978-1-939816-83-2
Printed in the United States of America

Cover design by Paula Ellenberger
www.paulaellenberger.com

10 9 8 7 6 5 4 3 2 1

This book is dedicated to my cherished friend, Colleen Hermanson. Your stalwart support for all my various efforts has done much to sustain me through the lean times. I just wish everyone could be blessed with a friend like you.

Once again I thank my husband, Joe Pivato, for carefully editing this manuscript, catching a number of typos and offering several good suggestions for improving it.

Finally, I thank my daughter, Juliana Pivato, for doing the final read through and catching even more typos and inconsistencies that I could not believe still existed!

It was coming straight at them, down the entrance ramp on the right. The huge wall of a tanker loomed on their left. Why was Gary driving so slowly? It was too late now anyway. The big white van was almost upon them, its GMC logo leering at her. Marion's last thought before it hit, before she lost all awareness, was "my poor daughter."

Chapter 1: Loss of Life—A new Life

Hilda Boaz hummed as she sautéed fish for supper, her slightly off-key notes covered by the roaring kitchen fan. Her husband should be back from driving her mother to the airport soon. *Maybe if we're alone for awhile it will help,* she thought. *Maybe if we have the chance to talk it through—to really talk it through—we'll get close again.*

Hilda stopped humming and turned the fan off. Had she heard something? Yes, there it was again—the doorbell. Who comes to the door at suppertime? "Somebody soliciting for money, no doubt," she muttered to herself. Hilda opened the door and stared in surprise at the two RCMP officers.

"Mrs. Boaz? Mrs. Thomas Garrett Boaz? Your mother is Marion McKay?" She nodded mutely. "I'm sorry to tell you that we have bad news for you. May we come in, please?" A while later, they left, turning with a final plea at the door. "Are you sure there's nobody we can call for you?"

"I have a cousin who lives nearby. I'll call him. He'll want to know."

But she didn't call. Bill wouldn't understand if she did—and he certainly couldn't help. He'd have his own loss to deal with when Claire finally explained it to him. And she'd have to be the one. Hilda and her autistic cousin were not close. They didn't even like each other.

Hilda sat down in her favorite living room chair, the half cooked fish forgotten on the cooling stove burner. She felt numb. *Shock,* she thought. Staring around the room, she suddenly realized *it's my room—my house now*. Her accountant's mind, so long attuned to adding up pluses and minuses, did a quick mental calculation of the financial implications of this sudden change of circumstance. Gary and she each had hefty life insurance policies. He'd insisted on that. And then there were Marion's assets. Hilda knew she was the chief beneficiary although she'd never actually seen the will. Marion had been rather secretive about that.

Hilda got up with the intention of going to Marion's room to find the will but then she collapsed back in her chair and the tears came for the first time. And they came hard. After several minutes, she recovered enough to think. She was alone. There was nobody left to care about her. And her poor mother had died an awful death. What had the officer said? That death had been instantaneous? That they couldn't have suffered? But there had to be those moments before. The horror of the inevitable—that van bearing down on them and nowhere to go—no escape.

Hilda scanned the room again. There, on top of the buffet, was their bottle of modestly-priced Scotch, the source of their nightly drink. And beside it sat the expensive cognac, saved for important guests—of whom they had few—and meted out sparingly by her

husband. *How many years had they had that bottle?*
Hilda wondered. She grabbed it along with one of the
three expensive brandy snifters they owned and
returned to her seat.

Hilda slopped a generous amount of brandy into her
glass, some spilling down the side and onto the table.
She laughed harshly, swiped it up with her hand and
wiped her hand down her dress. *How Gary would have
hated that*, she thought.

The waste, and the impropriety—but most of all the
waste!

Hilda continued to drink and ruminate well into the
night with each swallow reminding her of all they'd
passed up in their endless and single-minded quest for
money. She'd gone along with him on that, she had to
admit. It had been her father's obsession, too. But not
Marion's. She tried not to think of her mother because
every time she did, she was assaulted by an unbearable
onslaught of pain. No. She mustn't think of her. What
about the money? Where was she at now?

As the night progressed, Hilda's thoughts turned
more and more to her husband. And the anger grew.
He'd never liked Marion and he hadn't wanted her to
live with them. Marion threatened everything he
believed in. Hilda knew that. And it was worse since
Claire had started the group home. Marion had talked
endlessly of the challenges and the successes for the
three young adults who lived there, in the house across
the street from Claire's close friend Tia, and Tia's new
husband Jimmy, and Tia's precocious 10-year-old son
Mario.

Hilda thought about them, including her cousin, Bill.
He'd been very close to Marion in his own way and
soon he'd have to know...to know what happened. She
would call Claire tomorrow. Claire and Tia might not

care about *her* but they certainly cared about Marion and Bill.

Marion had been part of their little group from the beginning but Hilda had only been on the edge, partly her own choice and partly her husband's resistance. "What was the point of all this fussing over them?" he had asked. "It should be enough that they had a roof over their heads and food in their bellies." And once he'd even gone so far as to say that it was too bad they'd lived, particularly Jimmy's sister, Mavis, who was nonverbal and quadriplegic. What could she possibly get out of life?

But it wasn't all as pointless as Gary claimed. Hilda herself had seen the gains. She remembered Roscoe at Tia's wedding—how dignified he'd been, despite the fact that he had Down Syndrome. And how gracious he was to them during their first meal at his restaurant before it had officially opened. And what about Bill? According to Marion, he'd been doing well in his sous-chef job in the restaurant and becoming quite adept with a paring knife. *Who would have thought?* she asked herself. And then there was Mavis, Jimmy's sister. *Gary was right there to some extent*, Hilda thought. That really was a sad case. But she admired Tia and Jimmy for trying so hard to make a life for Mavis. *Like Claire with her daughter, Jessie,* Hilda thought. She was not convinced that either Jessie or Mavis was aware enough to even appreciate all the effort being expended on them.

But Marion—poor Marion! She'd been worried about Bill for so long, ever since she'd brought him up to Edmonton when she moved here. As his legal guardian, Marion had felt solely responsible for him. True, Jimmy had taken on co-guardianship when Hilda refused, but Marion had regarded that as just a technicality and continued to shoulder the burden alone.

And now that things were finally looking so good for Bill, Marion had thought she could take a trip back to Scotland to see the land where her parents grew up and connect with some cousins there. After a lifetime, she was finally going. And look what happened! Hilda wept again and this time she couldn't stop. She dragged herself from her chair and stumbled off to bed. It was already 3:30 in the morning. The bottle of cognac that had been three quarter's full that afternoon, was now three quarter's empty and it sat forlornly on the side table next to her chair.

Chapter 2: Hilda Hides

Hilda didn't open her eyes until 10:10 the next morning, a Monday—and when she did, she immediately closed them again. She had a monster headache but she knew she should call in to work. No. She would text, and then turn her phone off. She couldn't talk to anyone. She crafted a brief message in a necessarily telegraphic style since she could only really open one eye at a time and the light still hurt horribly.

Gary and my mom killed in car crash on way to airport yesterday. Please cancel or transfer all my appointments for the rest of the week. Day Timer on desk. Contact numbers listed.
Hilda.

After completing this mammoth task, Hilda used the washroom and crawled back into bed but she couldn't sleep. She crept out of bed to pull the curtains tighter against the morning light and then slipped back under the covers again. Lying there with her eyes closed, she tried to figure out how she was supposed to go on with her life. Marion's eager caring face, and Gary's often sour sneering one danced back and forth in front of her eyes. Waves of pain washed over her until gradually she fell into a restless sleep, the two aspirin she'd swallowed earlier finally taking effect.

When Hilda woke a second time, her mind was clearer. She deliberately put aside thoughts of Gary and Marion for the moment and tried instead to get in touch with who she was—or who she'd once been. Had she always been this focused on money, this uncaring of others? True, in the past couple of years, after Marion had threatened to cut Hilda out of her will, she'd become somewhat involved with the group, the Three Musketeers, as they and their restaurant were called. She'd handled the books and occasionally volunteered to help out at some function or other. She realized suddenly that there had been times that she'd actually enjoyed it, though her only reason for doing it had been to please her mother. But these pleasant memories had always quickly evaporated in the face of Gary's constant censure and negativity. He'd thought it was a waste of her time and completely pointless. And now?

What did she want? Who was she? What choices did she have? Hilda mulled these questions over and over. She looked around her empty bedroom. Like the rest of the house, it was clean, tidy, sparse and loveless. *How had they lived like this?* she asked herself. *Why? How could she live now?*

The house phone rang and jarred her out of her reverie. It rang a long time before it stopped. Hilda got up and put on the answering machine. Soon it rang again and she heard someone leaving a message. She tried to keep lying there in bed, a safe place, but the need for coffee was too strong.

Hilda got up and out of force of habit went through her usual morning routine, showering and dressing carefully in the power style that Gary had favored. She looked at herself in the mirror with distaste. *I'll go shopping somewhere where people don't know me and won't come around offering empty condolences as an excuse to get the inside story on what happened. Red Deer, maybe—or at least Leduc.* Leduc was a small city near the Edmonton International Airport.

When she was ready for the day and had consumed her first cup of black coffee, Hilda checked her answering machine. *Claire! Of course it had been Claire.* Hilda scrambled a couple of eggs and prepared some dry toast for herself, realizing that she was both hungry and queasy. She looked at the nearly empty brandy bottle distastefully. Drinking was clearly not the answer. However, it had gotten her through last night.

When she finally thought she had the strength to handle it, Hilda tried to call Claire back but the call wouldn't go through—"out of area" was the message she received. She called the operator for assistance and discovered that the call had come from Mexico. *Oh, yes, they were going there for Christmas,* Hilda remembered, and she asked the operator to patch her through. Claire answered the phone eagerly, seeing the call display. "Hilda, Hilda, Aunt Gus phoned me. She heard on the news. I'm so sorry. Tell me what we can do to help. We want to help you get through this!"

Hilda hesitated for a moment, not knowing how to respond. She had expected Claire to be ghoulishly pumping her for details—not to act instead like she actually cared. That was difficult to deal with. Hilda didn't care much about others and she found it difficult to believe that others could really care about her. What was Claire's game? Was she just being polite?

Claire interrupted Hilda's thoughts at this moment. "Please, Hilda. Let us help you. Do you need some company? Gus and Amanda could visit. And we need to discuss how to tell Bill." Claire's Aunt Gus and her friend, Amanda, were two retired ladies who lived next door to Tia and Jimmy and were part of the support group around Bill, Roscoe and Mavis.

"Uh, not yet. I'll be in touch," Hilda responded, and she hung up the phone quickly before Claire could object. Then she disconnected it. Next, she crafted a sign in large heavy letters on her computer, printed it out and stuck it securely to her front door with masking tape. It read "No Visitors Please".

Once all this was accomplished, Hilda sat down once more and drew the cognac bottle and her empty glass, still sitting there from the night before, closer to her. Although not normally a drinker, she was feeling that her only friend and her only solace at the moment lay in the bottle. Inside her a war was going on between the flashes of anger against her husband and the flashes of pain for the loss of her mother. The anger made her hot and dizzy and the pain made her weak, like she was drowning and dissolving and could not live through it.

An hour and a half later, the cognac bottle was empty and Hilda was just eying the Scotch, wondering what to do next, when the doorbell rang. She ignored it but it continued to ring mercilessly and finally she stumbled to the door, prepared to tell off whoever was there for having the gall to ignore her sign.

The same two officers who'd visited her the day before to tell her the terrible news were standing there. Hilda had no choice but to invite them in. She plunked herself back down in her chair and they sat down across from her, politely pretending not to notice the empty brandy bottle or the smell of alcohol on her breath. *What do I care what they think?* she asked herself angrily.

Chapter 3: What Really Happened

The officers reintroduced themselves as Rick Bradley and Georgia Cross. In the initial shock at their first encounter, Hilda hadn't even registered their names nor did she have any clear recollection of their faces. It was almost like meeting them for the first time.

"We've brought some personal items for you to identify," Rick said gently. "The crash was so severe it started a fire and I'm afraid there's not much left of the bodies."

Hilda winced and weaved slightly in her chair. Georgia rose and held out a strong hand to steady her. She murmured words of comfort. "The coroner said they must have died instantly. In fact, the autopsy revealed that your mother had the beginnings of a heart attack just before the accident. She may not even have been conscious when the collision occurred."

Hilda asked several questions about this, desperately wanting further affirmation. If only that was what had happened, she pleaded to she knew not whom. Hilda hadn't been to church for many years and always claimed to have no belief in God.

She stared at the large picture of her mother that now stood where the cognac bottle had previously been. Then her gaze shifted to the empty bottle itself. Her vision blurred and suddenly she saw it as the very symbol of Gary's meanness and acquisitiveness.

Rick and Georgia stared at her, concerned. Obviously, they were reading something in her face. Hilda just got up quietly, picked up the bottle and walked out to the kitchen. Then she hurled it as hard as she could into the stainless steel kitchen sink. It shattered readily into many pieces. She noted with regret that it made a small dent in the bottom of the sink but she simultaneously thought about how clever she'd been to break it there. This way she didn't have to pick up the broken pieces from all over the floor.

Hilda idly scraped a couple of pieces of glass into the sink from the edge of the counter where they'd landed, and in the process cut her finger. She didn't seem to notice, walked back into the living room dripping blood all the way, and plopped down in her chair. Georgia grabbed some Kleenex, gently wiped Hilda's finger, making sure there was no glass inside, and wrapped it in more Kleenex. Then she grabbed a stack of fresh Kleenex and mopped up the blood trail from the kitchen to the living room, pressing hard on the three drops of blood that had landed on the rug to get out as much as she could. Hilda just looked at her dumbly.

Rick had said nothing during all this time but now he turned to her and said gently, "We have grief counselors on staff. We could send one to your house— male or female, whoever you prefer."

"I'm fine," Hilda rasped. "All I need from you is to tell me exactly what happened. Whose fault was it?"

"It was a very unusual accident. It's not clear why it happened at all or why the two vehicles caught fire. Witnesses say that your husband was driving quite slowly, so slowly that a tanker truck was passing him in the left hand lane. The driver of the van was going very fast off the ramp and there's no evidence he slowed down at all or that your husband speeded up to avoid him. The van just slammed right into them and forced their car into the back wheels of the tanker truck. Because those tankers are so big, momentum kept it going. It broke free from the other two vehicles and came to a stop a few feet ahead, just beneath an overpass."

"But what about the fire?"

"It looks like it was your husband's car that caught fire and then engulfed the van. The firemen were afraid that the tanker truck would go too, and explode if it was carrying fuel. By the time they found out it was only a milk tanker and they could risk getting close enough to put the fire out, it was too late to save much of the other two vehicles. We'll know more when Forensics has completed their investigation. If the driver had any identification it was destroyed in the accident. Both vehicles are still being checked over to see if there were any mechanical defects."

Hilda put her hand to her mouth and then started rustling frantically through a pile of papers on the side table. "Oh, God!" she exclaimed, as she handed Georgia an official looking letter. "This arrived in the mail just a couple of days ago and I didn't even have a chance to tell Gary." Georgia read it out loud. It was a recall notice stating that the fuel line in Gary's car was placed too close to the rear axle and was at risk of causing a fire in case of a side crash.

"They could have taken my van," Hilda moaned. "My carelessness killed my mother!" Rick and Georgia glanced quickly at each other, noting the absence of any mention of Hilda's husband. "I'll bet it was that faulty fuel line!" Hilda said, her remorse suddenly turning to rage. "I'll sue!"

Rick replied, "You have two years to do that if it turns out to be the case. We don't really know yet why the accident happened the way it did. Once all the facts are in you can contact a lawyer if it comes to that."

Hilda nodded and slumped back into her chair, her lethargy returning. But in a moment she asked, "What about these possessions you mentioned?" Hilda thought of her mother's beautiful ruby and diamond ring that she'd always coveted. It had been a gift from Hilda's father on their 25th wedding anniversary and Marion had been wearing it when she left the house that last day. "My mother had a ring."

Georgia spread some Kleenex on the coffee table, opened up a large brown envelope and poured out the charred personal possessions of two lives. She held up the warped remains of a woman's ring, the gold partially melted and the stones blackened.

Hilda screamed when she saw it, the full horror of what must have happened washing over her. She ran to the washroom and threw up what little she'd eaten that morning. When she returned to the room she didn't sit down again but just yelled at them. "Take it away! Take it all away. And go! Leave me alone!"

Rick and Georgia got up. "Please, can we send someone to help you through this?" Georgia implored.

"I'm fine." Hilda choked, partially regaining her composure.

"What about that cousin you mentioned?" Rick asked.

"He's busy," Hilda said dully. Suddenly, she realized what they must be thinking. "Don't worry," she added. "I'm not suicidal."

After they left, Hilda sat down and methodically worked her way through what was left of the bottle of Scotch. Fortunately it was only one quarter full. Then she stumbled into the kitchen, grabbed a number of paper towels and cleaned the glass out of the sink and dumped it into the garbage. She became aware of a definite odor and registered the half cooked fish still sitting in the pan from the night before. She put it down the garbage disposal unit, noting, with a kind of warped amusement, the distinct grating sound of a couple of stray pieces of glass that must have fallen in. Then she opened the kitchen window and went to bed, even though it was only 8 o'clock.

Chapter 4: Out of the Ashes a New Life Begins

The next morning, Hilda awoke with another headache and a queasy stomach, although not as severe as the day before. A few minutes later, coffee in hand, along with a slice of lemon pie she'd found in the fridge, Hilda sat down in her living room with her usual selection of vitamin pills augmented by a B vitamin. She'd noticed that her hands were shaky from all her recent alcohol consumption.

"What am I going to do with the rest of my life?" Hilda asked herself. And, as she ate her pie and drank her coffee, she entered into a dream-like reverie.

What were the happy times? Various images flitted through her mind. She remembered visiting her father's parents on their farm near Red Deer as a little girl.

There had been a dog and two cats that roamed freely, in and out of the large rambling farmhouse. The dog was named Roxie for some reason and it had seemed to take a liking to Hilda, coming up frequently to nuzzle her hand as if asking for a back rub. Hilda knew that now but at the time she'd just pulled her hand away, afraid about germs. She'd always been afraid about germs. Well, no more! Hilda reached down and picked up a piece of piecrust that had fallen on the rug and deliberately ate it. "There!" she said triumphantly, although nobody was around to hear her.

Maybe I should get a pet! Hilda thought, and immediately considered how she could put her plan into action. *I'll be home this week so the time to do it would be now. I'll have four days or more to get it organized before I have to go back to work.* Hilda poured herself a big bowl of raisin bran, suddenly realizing how hungry she was. After finishing it and a second cup of coffee, she pulled out her laptop and searched for animal shelters in the area. But she didn't want to risk running into anyone she knew and was very pleased to discover that there was a shelter in Leduc.

The shelter website held an urgent plea for people to adopt. Apparently, an excess of stray dogs and cats had turned up recently and would have to be *put down* if people didn't come forward soon to claim them or adopt them.

Hilda grabbed her outside shoes, her purse and a sweater, locked up the house and headed towards Highway 2 South in her car. This was the road that led to the airport, Leduc and ultimately Calgary. She'd be passing the very spot where the accident had occurred and wondered if she'd recognize it and, if so, how she'd feel about that.

As it turned out, there was no problem with recognizing the area. The grass was charred on both sides of the road and there were still a few pieces of wreckage from the two vehicles lying in the ditch on the left hand side. Hilda recognized a strip of decorative molding from Gary's car with the distinctive line of angel wings. Her steering wheel wavered and she grasped it firmly with both hands and drove on slowly, her arms quivering. Just a short distance ahead was the first Leduc turn-off. She managed to turn the car onto the ramp and stop at a wide part in the road.

Hilda put her head down on the steering wheel and sat like that for several minutes. She felt sick and shaky and was afraid she might throw up. Suddenly, she remembered that the airport turn-off was just ahead. If only she hadn't asked Marion that last question at the door, holding them up that extra minute or two, they would've been at the turn-off and the accident would never have happened. She beat on the steering wheel and screamed aloud. Then she checked quickly and self-consciously to make sure the windows were closed and nobody was watching her.

After a couple of minutes, Hilda raised her head because a sudden thought had come into her mind. What can I do to be the daughter my mother wanted me to be, to be the person I started out to be? How can I atone for choosing my husband's path instead of her path? What would she want me to be doing now? Suddenly, Hilda realized that she knew the answer. For starters, she would want me to be happy—truly happy. Hilda put the car in gear and moved on, heading towards her new life.

Chapter 5: We Have Been Waiting for You

The Leduc Animal Rescue Society was large and noisy and smelly. Hilda took a step back in disgust and almost walked away. But the grey-haired woman at the desk raised her eyes from her computer and asked Hilda sweetly what she could do for her. There was something in her eyes and in the compassionate set of her face that reminded Hilda of Marion, and she sat down abruptly in a nearby chair and put her head down to hide her sudden tears. The woman came around the desk and stood before her. She put her hand tentatively on Hilda's shoulder and said to her, "You're suffering, aren't you, dear? You've lost someone."

Hilda raised her head, her eyes shiny with tears, and just nodded her head mutely.

"You come with me," the woman said. "We'll have a cup of tea and you can tell me why you're here and what you're looking for." Over her shoulder, she called out to someone in the back room. "Marcie, can you please take the desk for a few minutes?"

"Coming!" Marcie called back. And before Marcie could even reach the desk, the woman had spirited Hilda away to a small staff lunch room and sat her down at a table. She dropped a tea bag into a mug, filled it from a boiling water spigot and brought it back to the table already preset with cream, sugar and a tray of oatmeal cookies.

"You fix that up to suit yourself and I'll be right back with my cup," she said comfortingly, ignoring the tears now flowing freely down Hilda's face.

"I'm sorry," Hilda gasped when the woman returned. "I guess you remind me of my mother. She just died."

The woman said nothing but just waited.

Hilda looked at her kind face and the words suddenly just flowed out of her like a dam had been broken. Several minutes later, she ended by saying, "And I want to find my life again. I want to be the real me she saw and I refused to see. She always wanted a dog and I want to honor her memory that way." Hilda choked and finally came to a stop.

The woman said nothing for a moment, sensing that she must choose her words carefully. She wanted to help but she also had a responsibility to the animals under her care even though she knew in her heart that many of them would end up being destroyed for want of homes. Finally she began. "People say that you should not make any life changing decisions right after you've had such a tragic loss as you've suffered. Taking on a pet is a much bigger decision than most non-pet owners realize. Do you really feel you're prepared for such a big step?"

Hilda looked at her as if she felt betrayed and the woman hastened to add, "Look, I want to help you if I possibly can. I'll take you to see the animals scheduled for disposal this week because they've been here too long. If you choose one of them, you can take it home and if in a few days you change your mind, you can just bring it back. That way the animal will at least have a chance—and if it's upset by being returned, at least it won't have long to be upset."

Hilda's mind was not so hazed by grief that she missed the woman's meaning but she simply said, "I want to see them all. And I want to stay with them and talk to them as long as I need. And I want to be alone to do it. Is that possible?"

The woman looked at her again, her eyes large with wisdom and compassion. She knew people and she knew animals. This woman needed an animal and in the end, she would be good to an animal. The woman felt sure.

"I'll take you back," the woman said. She did so, and after she explained a few rules to Hilda about not banging on the bars or putting her hands in the cages she turned to leave.

"Wait!" Hilda called after her. "I don't even know your name!"

"Marion," she replied. "Marion Charles."

Hilda looked at her in shock. "Was I supposed to meet you, Marion?" she asked in a high, child-like voice.

"I believe so," Marion replied softly. And she left.

Chapter 6: Do You Really Want Me?

Hilda spent a long time walking back and forth among the cages. The woman had unlocked the doors separating the various sections and pointed out to her the groups of dogs and cats designated for disposal in the coming week or two. Hilda tried to harden her heart, to tell herself that if she was going to take on any animal it had to be the best one for her, but she kept coming back again and again to that section.

There was a cat there. It wasn't cute like some of the others and it didn't look like much. Hilda passed by to look at the rest of the cats again. There were among the mix a few Persians and even a Siamese. Her acquisitive side urged her to get one of these if she was going to get a cat at all. She could tell the few acquaintances she had who might eventually visit her that she'd gotten it from a breeder, not through an animal shelter. It wouldn't sound so pathetic that way.

Hilda returned yet again to visit the cat and promised herself that this would be the last time. She looked at the cat and the cat looked at her but made no effort to approach. Instead he—or she—seemed to pull back, to raise its head in defiance. But when she did catch it looking at her, she saw something else in its eyes. It was a longing, as if it wanted someone to trust and belong to. Hilda shook herself. *I'm just reading into the situation*, she thought, but she went back to the office area to ask Marion about the cat. Marion returned with her and this time she felt the sense of shock that Hilda had felt when she first heard her name.

"I've been upset about that cat," she said. "From what I've seen of her, I think she's very intelligent, and has deeper feelings than a lot of cats. She acts like she wants somebody to love, to be part of a family, and that's not often the case with cats. They tend to be users, charming as they can be!"

"But I'm not a family. I'm just alone."

"You can make a family," Marion said softly. "You mentioned the people in your life, the young people in the home. I bet they would enjoy having a cat around at times!"

"I don't know," Hilda responded. "I came here for a dog. I don't know why I'm even looking at cats."

"Okay," Marion said, after a slight pause. "Let's go back and look at the dogs."

They walked back and forth along the rows of cages housing the dogs—the dogs that would be staying a while longer and hopefully be adopted, and the dogs that had been there awhile and would soon be ending their lives. Hilda looked into their faces, one after another, trying to recall Roxie, her only point of reference. They toured *death row*, as Hilda had taken to calling it, a second time and finally, at the very end of the row, she saw something in the dog there that made her want to know him better.

"What is he?" she asked.

"They don't come to us with a pedigree but the last time the vet was in he speculated that he was a cross between a black lab and a fox terrier."

"A big dog then—and a mutt."

"Not necessarily," Marion said in a controlled, even voice. She recognized the note of snobbery in Hilda's response but thought it was better not to respond to it. "He's reached his full adult size at this point. The vet speculates he's between two and three years old. And he seems intelligent and sensitive." As an afterthought she added, "Black labs are known for their loyalty."

"Can I put my hand through the cage? Will he bite?"

"Go ahead. He's shown no signs of violence and we've had him here for over a month now."

Hilda waved her hand around with no response from the dog until Marion suggested that she keep it still and just be patient. In a couple of minutes, the dog came over to her and sniffed her hand. Then he looked her full in the face and Hilda thought she read a resigned look in his eyes as if he knew what was coming, as if he wanted to be wanted but could not beg. That was not who he was.

Hilda coughed to cover a sudden uprising of emotion in her chest. She knew what it was to feel that way but she'd forgotten somehow—or papered over that feeling along the way. She tentatively stroked the top of his head and he leaned into her hand. "How long does he have?" she asked Marion.

"He's overdue already. Some time this week for sure."

Hilda caressed him under the chin and he looked her fully in the eye. She thought suddenly that she could probably forge a deeper emotional connection with him than she'd had with her late husband. He seemed more real, more present somehow. "Can he come out?" she asked Marion.

Marion fetched a leash hanging on a nearby peg and, reaching into the cage, she connected it to his collar and drew him out. The dog stood obediently at her feet waiting for directions. "Do you want to take him for a walk?" Marion asked.

"No. I just want to be alone with him for a few minutes. Would that be okay?"

Marion said nothing but fetched a chair for Hilda. "I'll be out front if you need me. Just push this bell

when you're through and want to put him back." She
turned in the direction of the office and soon Hilda and
the dog were all alone. He sat quietly at her feet and she
ran her hand up and down his back. Gradually she
began talking to him, telling him what had happened.
He licked her hand in solace as if he understood.

After some minutes, Hilda turned the conversation,
the monologue really, to why she wanted a dog. She
told him what she could not tell anyone else, how
lonely she felt, how guilty she felt over how she'd
treated her mother, how unhappy she'd been with her
late husband without even realizing it, how out of touch
she was with herself. The dog continued to listen to her,
licking her hand occasionally when he heard a break in
her voice.

After about 15 minutes of this, Hilda called Marion
who came almost immediately. "Do you want me to put
the dog back?" she asked.

"No. You remember that cat? Could you bring it
here? Would that be okay?"

Marion looked at the dog. She recognized
immediately that a bond was forming between him and
Hilda and she struggled to keep the tears out of her own
eyes. "I'll see what I can do," she said, more gruffly
than she'd intended, and turned away quickly.

Within three minutes, she was back carrying the cat
in a net. The cat was meowing querulously. "Hold onto
the dog's collar firmly. I'm going to dump the cat out
on the floor. She can't go far since both ends of this
hallway are locked off but don't try to grab her. Let her
come to you and the dog if she will. She may have had
bad experiences with dogs before and the time to find
that out would be now."

Marion dumped the cat out and it raced away to the
end of the hall. The dog looked curious but made no
effort to go after her. Marion said, "I'm going to go out

that door and just watch through the window. I'll be right there if you need me." And with that she left.

Hilda sat immobile. She felt rather overwhelmed by the situation but she also felt her heart filling in a way she did not recognize. She sat inert, occasionally stroking the dog, and he too did not move. Gradually the cat moved closer but Hilda did nothing. Somehow she knew that trying to entice her would only drive her away. If the cat were prepared to accept the situation she would come to Hilda in her own time.

Another quarter hour passed and Marion realized that it was closing time. She went to the front to say good-bye to Marcie and locked the door behind her. When she returned to her window post, she saw that the cat had climbed into Hilda's lap and the dog had placed a paw on her knee. The cat didn't seem to mind. Marion pulled out her cell phone and took some pictures. She hoped they turned out because she couldn't really see clearly through the blur of her tears.

This is what it's all about, she thought. There they are—three lost souls coming together like a family. What could be better than this?

Marion opened the door and stood quietly just inside. "Well?" she asked.

"How do I get them home?" Hilda asked. "And what do I feed them?"

"I can sell you a leash for the dog and a litter box for the cat. I can give you a cardboard crate for the cat and a couple of day's worth of food for both of them. We have written instructions available on providing appropriate care and I'll give you a list of websites and YouTube sites you can consult. Do you have any friends who are animal owners who could help you out?"

"I know a couple of ladies who have cats," Hilda said tentatively.

"That's good. I think the cat will be the bigger challenge. She's a little temperamental. There were many more docile ones you could have chosen— although I'm glad this particular one will have a home."

Chapter 7: Homeward Bound

Somehow Hilda made it home. She alternated between shaking her head over what she'd done and feeling her heart soar over the thought that she was not going home to an empty house. The dog lay quietly on the floor of the front passenger seat and the cat squealed indignantly within the confines of her cardboard cage on the back seat.

When she arrived home, Hilda quickly released the dog into her fully-fenced back yard. Then she carried the cat into the kitchen, closing off the hall and living room doors before releasing her. She set up the litter box in the adjoining powder room and laid out a bowl of water and a bowl of cat food in a corner of the kitchen. Then she left the cat to her own devices and went in search of the dog.

When Hilda opened the back door she noted that the dog was just completing his business in a corner of the yard so that took care of one problem. *It would now be safe to have him in the house for the night*, she thought. Hilda laid a folded blanket down near the back door in the utility room and called the dog in. "Lay down," she said, and he lay down obediently. Marion had told her that the dog's behavior indicated he'd had a kind owner before and had learned basic manners. He seemed to know what was expected of a housedog and Hilda breathed a sigh of relief.

Hilda put out food and water for him and watched him eat a little and drink gratefully. Then she returned to the cat. She found her lounging contentedly on top of the fridge! "How did you get up there?" she sputtered. "You can't do that. That's unsanitary!" Hilda grabbed at the cat to get her down and received a nice long scratch on her arm for her trouble. "Fine, stay there!" she said. "What do I care anyway? There's nobody around anymore to criticize my housekeeping!"

Hilda opened the door from the kitchen to the utility room where the dog was settled, to see if he'd bother the cat. But he took no notice of her. She said good night to her new companions and went off to bed, leaving the doors between the kitchen and bedroom open.

The next morning, Hilda woke at eight to find the dog's wet nose pushing at her hand. "What? Oh," she said and got up to let him out the back door. The cat, noticing that she was up, meowed imperiously and Hilda went to fill her food bowl and freshen her water. "Roxie!" Hilda exclaimed. "*Roxie* is a name that will suit you. It has a rough edge to it, like you. And I can't call the dog Roxie because it's a female name. So *Roxie* it is. Get used to it!"

Hilda thought of her mother then, and for the first time she felt a sense of warmth instead of cold despair. Her mother would be pleased at what Hilda had done to acquire her new companions. She felt sure of that. Her mother had liked animals, but her father had never wanted to have any around.

Hilda heard a small *arf* at the door and walked over to let the dog in. *He was a very polite dog*, she thought––and a little on the timid side. A name for him would come to her, she knew, but it hadn't come yet. She fixed up his food and water bowl, chattering away to him as she did so. It felt good to have someone to talk to who wouldn't criticize her for what she said. Of course, she'd always been able to talk to Marion but they were very different people with different interests, never really on the same page.

Once she'd finished her own breakfast, Hilda thought about what she would do that day. "Nothing," was her answer—and she certainly wouldn't be drinking! *That had been a one-off*, she thought—and it wasn't necessary any more. Now, when things built up inside her to an unbearable level she had somebody to talk to, to cry in front of. She thought about phoning Gus and Amanda to tell them about the cat and the dog but decided against it. Instead, she checked out the sites on *YouTube* that Marion Charles had recommended and she and the animals spent many contented hours together just watching them and getting used to each other.

Chapter 8: Healing

The next three days passed the same way. At one point there was a determined pounding at the door but, fortunately, Hilda had all the lights out at the time as it was mid-afternoon and she pretended not to be home. *I don't want people*, she thought. I have my companions now.

Hilda still had helpless crying spells when she could not seem to stop. At those times, the dog always came over to sit beside her and often he'd put his paw on her knee. One day, as she was looking down at him, she knew what his name had to be: *Job*, as in the Biblical Job—patient, resigned and ever faithful. (For those of you a generation or more removed from the Bible, it's pronounced *Jobe*).

Roxie and Job, she thought—my new companions! Marion Charles had warned her about what an adjustment it would be to be a pet owner and about how much there was to learn, but Hilda had not found it hard. For example, she had not made a big deal about Roxie's frequent need to escape to the top of the fridge and be alone. She understood it, actually, since she felt the same way and still had the *No Visitors* sign on her door. Also, she was naturally an early riser and had no difficulty accommodating Job's early morning need to go outside. But the biggest factor in the startling success of their easy adjustment to each other was Hilda's state of malaise.

Hilda's intense grief had made her lethargic. She didn't care about much and sat around for hours at a time, the dog at her feet and the cat in her lap—when Roxie felt like sitting there. She fed them and tended to their needs dutifully, including a daily walk with Job. This little bit of structure provided some shape to her life and it was all the structure she could tolerate at the moment. She ate when she was hungry and when her food supply and the food for the animals provided by the shelter ran low, she contacted a friend at work, Jack Shaw, an odd bird like herself.

He was the one person she knew who wouldn't ask questions and wouldn't push. Her email to him read as follows: "You will have heard. I need some items from the food store—see below. Email approximate arrival time and amount due and leave the items on the front step. I will leave the money in the mailbox. Do not ask to come in. I am not receiving at present. Regards, Hilda." Her list followed and included the names of the dog and cat foods and the required amounts. She sent the email at 10 in the morning and by 5:30 that evening she had the required items. Jack had rung the doorbell when he arrived and by the time she peeped out the window to see who was there, he'd gone.

The only other contact Hilda had during that time was from Marion Charles who sent her an email when she couldn't get through on the phone. Hilda responded that all was well and said she'd be in touch in a week or so. And that was it. For a solid week, she lived outside the world, trying to sew up the giant gap in her life so that she could find a way to go on. It seemed to Hilda that the dog felt her pain—and the cat recognized and respected it.

It was now Sunday night, exactly a week since her husband and mother had died, and Hilda was trying to decide whether she could or should go back to work the next morning. She was beginning to feel restless at home but still felt very quivery and unsettled. Finally, she decided to phone Jack, her one *friend* at work, the one who'd dropped off the food. He answered the phone after several rings and Hilda didn't bother to say hello. She asked instead, "Are they surviving there without me?"

"I took on your appointments. A couple of them grumped but I told them to stuff it."

Hilda gave a faint chuckle. "I hope they weren't rich clients," she said, but even as she said it she found she didn't care all that much anymore.

"You have only two appointments in your calendar for this week which I can cover—and the secretary isn't accepting any more bookings for you until further notice. If you want to take another week off, why don't you do that?"

"I don't know. I have to think about it. I don't know what I want. If I'm not there by 10 tomorrow morning, just tell Janice I'm not coming in this week."

"Will do. I guess I'll see you when I see you. Text me if you need anything. Night!"

Hilda did not respond but just hung up the phone. She felt better—connected but not too connected. Just the way she liked it. She'd decide tomorrow morning what to do. For sure, Job would get her up early enough.

Chapter 9: Starting Over

The next morning, Hilda stumbled out of bed in response to Job's wet nose pushing against her hand. She fed Roxie and put on some coffee. Then she sat down in her favorite chair to think. For a moment, old worries poured into her head. It was a competitive business. What if some of her clients decided they liked working with Jack better than with her? What if those who couldn't get an immediate appointment decided to go elsewhere?

Hilda realized with a start that she wasn't sure she even wanted to go back to work—ever. She was tired of dealing with affluent clients and their first world problems. She did a quick financial calculation and realized that she didn't have to return if she didn't want to. That did it. She felt better—and knew she needed to take this week off in order to have time to decide what to do.

Hilda was satisfied with her decision but she still felt restless. What should she do? She wandered into Marion's room and slowly surveyed it. She noted with sadness the various bits of Scottish memorabilia Marion had collected through the years. On one wall, a tea towel inscribed with Scottish recipes had been mounted in an inexpensive frame. It featured something called Cullen Skink, as well as Cock-a-Leekie stew and Oatmeal Scones.

In a bookshelf on the wall beside the tea towel, Hilda spotted a Scottish Bagpiper doll, and a Scottish teapot rested its bottom on a matching cup of equal size. She had never understood the point of that. On a lower shelf, Hilda spied two Scottish cookbooks and a couple of cds: *Blazin' Fiddles* and the *Cairn String Quartet*. On the remaining wall space, a line of crested Scottish teaspoons took pride of place.

Hilda sat down in Marion's paisley, high-backed Scottish armchair, the one piece of furniture Marion had brought with her when she came to live with Hilda, and wept. Marion had wanted this trip so much, dreamt of it for so long. It wasn't fair!

Presently, Hilda composed herself and regarded a stack of detective stories on the side table next to the chair. Hilda had always sneered at Marion's reading tastes, telling her she should read something useful like financial magazines that could provide her with tips for her investment portfolio. She scanned the titles, recognizing some of Marion's favorites. They were all detective stories featuring well-known characters: Agatha Christie's Miss Marple, Ruth Rendell's Inspector Wexford and Donna Leon's Commissario Guido Brunetti. Hilda carried the books back to her bedroom and crawled back into bed, a fresh batch of tears running down her face.

After she recovered, Hilda flicked idly through the books but couldn't really get into any of them. She got up and dressed and then wandered into the living room. The first thing that struck her was Gary's fancy black leather chair sitting there. Since Roxie had arrived, Hilda had stopped her a half a dozen times from using the chair to sharpen her claws, but she still noticed a couple of small scratches on the back of it.

Hilda sat down in the chair and the phone rang. She had finally reconnected it the night before. Hilda picked it up to discover it was a Dr. Gelrose from the coroner's office. They were through with the bodies and wondered what she wanted done with them. Hilda gulped—sentiment and money sense, love and hate at war in her brain.

"I was told they were burnt beyond recognition. Is that true?"

The caller affirmed this.

"I suppose it's best to cremate them then. What do I do?"

"We can send the bodies to the crematorium but it will be your responsibility to pay the costs. We can give them your contact information."

Illogically, Hilda felt like arguing with him, saying they should pay the costs, but then she stopped herself. "Could I see them before they are sent off?"

"There isn't much to see," he said kindly. "I suggest you just remember them how they were."

"When are you sending them?"

"We have a truck going out today."

Hilda gulped and closed her eyes. "Okay," she said weakly. "Send them." And she hung up the phone abruptly.

Hilda sat for a while coping with a fresh onslaught of tears. Then she wriggled around in Gary's chair and thought to herself, *I hate this chair—and I am tired of arguing with the damn cat over it!* She looked around the room at her nice blue sofa set and said, "I think I'll get another recliner—smaller, in my size, and cloth covered, some tough material that does not snag easily. I'll get it in a soft brown color maybe. People say that blue and brown don't go together but I don't care." *All the more reason to get brown*, she thought rebelliously.

Suddenly, Hilda remembered one of her mother's last concerns before she died. She'd wanted to get Bill a nice, comfortable recliner like the one Gary had.

Roscoe had a recliner and Mavis had her nice reclining wheelchair. Only Bill had no chair to relax his legs in. *Well, now he shall have one!* Hilda thought triumphantly, and she picked up the phone and called her neighbor.

Chapter 10: Hilda Comes Back to the World

"Hello. Mary here," came the prim voice over the phone.

"Mary, it's Hilda."

"Oh, Hilda! How…"

"Is Bob home? I'd like some help loading a chair into my van."

"We'll be right over!" Mary gushed. "You poor…"

"Thanks," Hilda said curtly, and hung up the phone.

Bob and Mary arrived within minutes. Hilda greeted them briefly and said, "I'd appreciate help with putting that chair in my van," and she pointed at the luxurious leather recliner that dominated her living room.

"Oh!" Mary gasped. "I hope you're not giving that to one of those charity outfits. The people who get furniture from there would not appreciate it."

Hilda recognized the acquisitive note in Mary's voice because she'd often felt that way herself. "No," she said coolly. "I'm taking it to my cousin. Of course, he's severely autistic and not really capable of appreciating its quality. But I'm sure he'll enjoy sitting in it, which is the main thing, don't you agree?"

Mary nodded her head mutely. Bob said, "You have one of those vans with the hide away seats, right? If you give me your keys, I can bring it out and put the seats down if you like?"

Hilda thanked him and handed him the keys. She strode to the back door and pushed the garage door opener. She decided that she liked him better than Mary.

When Bob left, Mary started in, "Now tell me, dear, what…" but Hilda cut her off.

"I don't want to talk about it!" An awkward silence followed until Bob came back in.

"The car's all ready. Who's going to help me carry it out?"

"I will," Hilda said, and immediately applied herself to wrestling with the chair. As she did so, a letter fell out from where it had slipped down in the side. Mary picked it up but Hilda dropped the chair and snatched it from her, taking it and leaving it in her bedroom and closing the door firmly behind herself when she came out.

After they got the chair loaded, Mary headed out to get in the van. Hilda said, "I have people there who can help me unload. I want to stay and visit with my cousin for a while. My mother was his guardian and he's likely to be pretty upset. Thanks for your help," she added, dismissively.

"Oh!" Mary said. Bob just raised his eyebrows, gave Hilda a little grin and left. Mary followed him reluctantly. Hilda had no intention of telling Bill what had happened to Marion but Mary did not need to know that. She thought she might head south after dumping off the chair—maybe go to some mall where she was unlikely to run into anybody she knew and just do a little clothes shopping.

Chapter 11: Cracks in the Ice

Hilda was so anxious to get away from Bob and
Mary that she didn't want to stop and phone ahead to
the house. She just hoped somebody was there to take
the chair, but after she backed into the driveway and
rang the bell, a strange woman came to the door.

"Uh, is Claire here?" Hilda asked.

"No. She's still in Mexico. They'll be back Friday.
I'm Eva, one of the assistants. Can I help you?"

"Oh, well, I'm Hilda, Bill's cousin. I just wanted to
drop off a recliner for him that my mother promised."

"Oh?" Eva said. "I never heard anything about that!"
The two of them stood there looking at each other
suspiciously. "I'm sorry," Eva added after a pause. "I'll
need to see some identification before I can admit you.
Those are the rules."

Meanwhile, across the street, Gus, Claire's aunt, was
staring out the window taking the scene in. "Amanda,
come and see this! Hilda is visiting the house!"

Amanda stepped quickly to the window. "Oh!" she
said.

Gus was already moving towards the door. "I better
go over there and talk to her!" she said.

"Wait, Gus! I talked to Claire this morning on the
phone. She asked me to talk to Hilda first. I'm sorry."

"Oh!" Gus said, a hurt look on her face.

"It's tricky," Amanda added. "You know we tried to
visit but she wasn't letting anybody in and you saw that
No Visitors sign on her door. Claire thinks she must be
a little unbalanced right now and would need calm, dull

people around her who don't ask questions. That would be me, not you!"

"Fine," Gus said, resignedly. "I have no idea how someone would feel under those circumstances. But you *will* tell me everything she says, won't you?"

"I promise," Amanda said, and quickly left. "Hey, Hilda!" she called, as she crossed the street.

Hilda turned to her in confusion, recognition dawning slowly. "I brought a recliner for Bill. She won't let me in."

"She doesn't know you. She's new." Amanda turned to Eva and said, "It's okay. This is Bill's cousin."

Eva opened the door and Hilda glared at her. "I need help to get the chair out."

Eva glanced down the street. "Oh, there are the guys. They went with Barry, one of our new assistants, to the restaurant for a snack. Roscoe wanted some coconut cream pie. I see they brought a whole pie back!'

The guys approached and Hilda said a curt *hello*, then returned quickly to her van and threw the back gate open. She beckoned to Barry and Bill. "Here, Bill, this is for you."

Bill looked in the back of the van. "Why?"

"Because."

"That Gary chair. Why…?"

"Gary won't…"

Amanda grabbed Hilda's arm before she could finish. She beckoned to Barry and said, "Please get the chair in and then lock up the car and bring the keys over." She pulled Hilda by the elbow. "Come on, Hilda. I have something to tell you."

Hilda resisted at first but then allowed herself to be led across the street. Amanda took her around to the back of the house, opened the kitchen door and beckoned her in.

Hilda walked up the three steps to the kitchen and sat down heavily in one of the kitchen chairs. When Amanda saw Gus peeking in from the living room, she scowled at her fiercely and motioned her away. Then she sat down at the table. "Coffee?" she asked, "or tea?"

"Uh, maybe juice if…"

Amanda pulled some apple juice out of the fridge as well as an open bottle of white wine. She grabbed two small glasses and poured some juice. "Let's start with this and maybe move on," she said, motioning at the wine.

Hilda gave her a wan smile and accepted the glass of juice.

"Bill doesn't know yet," Amanda said. "Claire's not here. She and Tia and their husbands left for Mexico the Friday before Marion was supposed to leave."

"Oh, uh. I knew she'd gone there but I thought she'd be back by now. She called me."

"Yes. Gus called her to let her know. We tried to call but you had your phone off the hook. Then we tried to visit but you had a big sign on your door."

"Was that you pounding?"

"Gus. She was worried."

"Where is she?"

Gus came around the corner then, from where she'd obviously been listening. She was carrying her big Persian cat in her arms. "Here," she said. "Hold Waldorf. He understands a lot."

Gus stood there, anxiously waiting to see what would happen, but Hilda just grabbed the cat, held him up to her chest and buried her face in his fur. Mercifully, he did not scratch her, although Gus could not imagine him tolerating such familiarity under normal circumstances.

Gus sat down then and said, "Waldorf is an exceptional cat. My other one, Salatta, wouldn't have understood. He's sorry. I'm sorry. I liked Marion. I don't like everyone." Gus got up, grabbed a glass and poured herself a healthy slug of wine. Then she sat down again, this time staying quiet.

"Let's move!" Amanda said. "This is not comfortable."

Hilda got up awkwardly, still holding onto Waldorf, and Amanda led her to a comfortable cloth recliner in the living room, sat her down and pulled the knob to lean the chair back. She grabbed a blanket and put it over Hilda's legs and then brought their glasses and the wine bottle out. She scooped up one of her cats and sat down in another recliner and put the seat back.

"Waldorf doesn't tolerate strangers usually. He likes you, for some reason," Gus said to Hilda. She was perched on the very edge of the sofa peering intently at Hilda. Amanda just shook her head.

"Maybe he smells my cat."

"You have a cat?"

"Yeah. And a dog, too."

"When did that happen?" Amanda asked.

Hilda looked confused. She had lost any clear sense of time. "I don't know….a week…maybe longer……..a few days after…"

"Where from?" Gus asked.

"Leduc…a shelter…..they were going to die…..all going to di-i-e," and Hilda put her head down and started to cry. Waldorf jumped down and stalked away to a quiet corner, situating himself beneath a stray sunbeam from the late afternoon sun.

Gus started to get up and opened her mouth, but Amanda shook her head and held her finger to her lips, motioning for her to sit back down and stay quiet.

In a minute, Hilda raised her head and asked, "Will Claire be back soon?"

"Three more days," Amanda replied. "She wants to arrange a memorial service for Marion. Would that be okay?"

"What happened to the bodies?" Gus blurted out.

"They burnt... they all burnt up—so he sent them to the crematorium. I guess they are there," and Hilda gasped, remembering the ring.

"We can get the cremains for you if you like," Amanda said, desperately trying to smooth over the moment. "Or you can come with us and pick out some urns."

"I don't know," Hilda replied.

"I'd wait," Gus said gruffly, now in touch with Hilda's pain. "They aren't going anywhere. Claire will know what to do."

Chapter 12: Claire Commiserates; Tia Moderates

This time when the doorbell rang, Hilda answered. The dog stood beside her, alert and wary. In the ten days he'd been with Hilda, he'd gradually taken on a protective role. Job could see that she needed watching over.

"Come in," Hilda said flatly when she opened the door. Claire reached forward impulsively to give her a hug but Hilda took a step back. Tia's response was more measured. She held out her hand and said softly, "We're so sorry, Hilda." Hilda took her hand briefly and then let it drop but this gesture had somehow thawed her a little. "Come into the living room."

After they settled themselves, the dog sat down beside Hilda. "This is Job," Hilda said. "He's my new manager." The cat peeped in cautiously from the doorway. "And that's Roxie. "We have an understanding. She puts up with my moods and I put up with hers."

Claire felt relieved that Hilda was able to joke a little. She'd never been comfortable dealing with other people's intense emotions.

"What can I get you?" Hilda asked, perfunctorily.

"Oh…" Claire started.

"We just had something, thanks," Tia said smoothly. "Can we just talk?"

Hilda said nothing and Claire waited helplessly for Tia to take over. "Can you tell us about it?" Tia added.

"They were on their way to the airport. A big van came shooting out from an off-ramp right at them.

There was a tanker truck in the left lane and the van rammed them right into it. The two cars caught fire. There was a recall because of a faulty fuel line in Gary's car but we'd just gotten the notice."

"Were they still alive when the fire…?" Claire asked, not daring to finish the sentence. Tia winced.

"No, the officers don't think so," Hilda responded curtly.

"Thank you for telling us what happened," Tia said in a conclusive tone. "Have you had time to think what you're going to do now?"

Hilda seemed to respond to Tia's calm manner and told them the story about acquiring the animals and about Marion Charles. Meanwhile, Roxie had circled around the room and finally settled in Tia's lap. From her new perch, Roxie stared at Claire and Claire thought, *she feels my tension.* Hilda looked at the cat and reached her hand down to nervously stroke the dog's head.

Tia broke the growing tension by commenting, "Marion and I talked about pets once, when she visited me, and Amanda came over with one of her cats. I remember her saying that she liked animals. She also said that she wished you and Gary would get a pet. It might help to calm you down a bit."

"She said that?" Hilda asked eagerly. "When I made my decision I felt like she would approve." Hilda put her head down then to hide a sudden surge of emotion but an escaping tear betrayed her.

Claire couldn't take the tension throbbing beneath the surface of this visit any longer. She felt overwhelmed by a powerful need to help. "What now, Hilda? When are you going back to work?"

"Maybe I won't," she said. "Or maybe not there…I have to think."

"I thought you liked accounting work."

"Do you have to *like* just one thing?" Hilda asked, a faint note of sarcasm in her voice. Tia winced.

"No," Claire said thoughtfully, relieved that she'd finally found a possible avenue for relating to Hilda. "I really loved interior decorating but the satisfaction I've gotten out of running the home for Roscoe and Bill and Mavis is on a whole different level."

"Why do you think that is?" Hilda asked, seeming genuinely interested.

"I don't know," Claire said slowly. "It's intellectually satisfying—but so is interior design in a certain way. "But with that I always wondered what the people would do with it after I was gone—and with this, I have the chance to see how my ideas work out for people."

"H-m-m," was all Hilda said in response.

They talked a little more and then Tia said, "Well, I guess it's time we were going," shuffling in her chair and dislodging the cat.

"But let me ask you, Hilda," Claire blurted. "Is there any chance it wasn't an accident?"

Tia held her breath but then Hilda gave a surprising response. "Yes," she said. Georgia, one of the police investigators, called me this morning. She said that Gary's brake cable was frayed."

"But, anyway, it was the other car that hit them!" Tia pointed out. "And I gather it didn't even slow down!"

"Well, let's get back to Gary for a minute," Claire said, suddenly feeling a bit more in her element now that they were dealing with facts rather than emotions. "Did he have any troubles with anybody? Had he said anything about anybody bothering him?"

"No-o-o," Hilda replied slowly. "He was always on the secretive side and preoccupied with his work—and I didn't know what he was really thinking a lot of the time." She remembered the letter that had dropped out of Gary's chair but said nothing.

"But the brake cable?" Tia asked.

"He did tend to ride the brakes when he drove," Hilda explained. "Maybe that's all that it was—normal wear and tear."

"But there are certainly some unanswered questions," Claire persisted. "Are they going to be looking into it further?"

"I don't know," Hilda said softly, and put her head down again.

"Okay, we're going to leave now," Tia stated firmly, getting up. "Is there anything we can do for you, Hilda? Shopping? Cleaning? Anything you need? And Gus and Amanda asked if they could visit and meet your pets?"

"I don't know," Hilda responded wearily, getting up herself. "I have a car. I'll call you if I think of anything." And with that, she walked them to the door, Job at her side.

Chapter 13: Murder by Accident

"Well, what do you think, Claire?" Tia asked. They had gone back to Claire's home to discuss their visit. They knew that if they went to Roscoe's home or Tia's home, Gus would be right over to find out what had happened and they wanted the chance to talk it through alone first.

"I don't know," Claire said slowly. "It could have been an accident, I guess."

"I mean, what did you think about Hilda? Is she doing okay?"

"I've always found it hard to read her. She's pretty private." Claire thought for a minute and then added, "I think the fact that she got the animals and seems to have adjusted to them so well is a healthy sign."

"I wonder why she did that?" Tia mused.

"Like she said, Marion would have approved. Hilda was kind of nasty and judgmental towards Marion. Maybe she feels guilty now."

"Sad," Tia commented. "How do you think she's feeling about losing her husband?"

"She hardly mentioned him," Claire responded. "I don't think they had much of a relationship. The few times I saw them together they didn't seem very close."

"She said she's not sure about going back to work. I wonder what that's about."

"It seems like she's doing some major reassessing of her life, like it's something she needs to do on her own. I guess we shouldn't interfere too much."

"I think I made it clear to her that she could call us any time and I think she believed me. Maybe I can just casually invite her for dinner in about a week and you can do the same some time?" Tia suggested.

"We're not exactly close friends with her. I think it would seem funny. I'm more interested in following up on the discrepancies in the accident that she mentioned. I think that would be the best way we could help her. What if somebody was out to get rid of Gary—and Marion was just collateral damage?"

"Well, even if that's true, there's not much to go on. According to Hilda, the bodies were burnt beyond recognition. The firemen were afraid the tanker truck was going to explode so they didn't even try to put the fire out and they couldn't douse it from the air because it was right near the overpass."

"But it said on the news that the tanker was actually carrying milk, not gas."

"Sure, but by the time they found that out, it was too late."

"I'd still like to follow up. I think I'm going to call Hilda back and ask if she has Gary's computer at home."

"That's sort of pushy. It might have a lot of private stuff on it. And what would his computer have to do with it, anyway?"

"Maybe he was into something he shouldn't have been. Anyway, we have to start somewhere!"

"Or not," Tia said, sighing. "I'm almost eight months pregnant at this point. I could do without another mystery right now."

"I'm going to call and ask her anyway," Claire said stubbornly. The phone rang then and their conversation came to an end. It was Gus calling to find out if they were back yet and what Hilda had had to say.

Chapter 14: Claire Gets to Work

Claire had the next day off and she called Hilda. After the initial greetings she asked, "Hilda, you mentioned that Gary had been very secretive lately."

"He was always that way—but, yes, more so lately."

"Have you thought to check his e-mail to see if anybody was threatening him? Did he bring his computer home with him from work?"

"Yes, it's here but I haven't looked at it. What for?"

"If it wasn't an accident, don't you want to know what happened?"

"Not particularly. What good would it do? They'd still be dead!"

Claire gulped and then went on bravely. "It sounds to me from what you said yesterday that you still have some unfinished business with your husband. Wouldn't it help to know who he really was?" Claire knew that if Tia had heard this brash remark she'd have been appalled, so she waited breathlessly to see if Hilda would answer her or just hang up the phone. The silence stretched.

Finally, Hilda said, "Maybe I don't want to know. Maybe it's better this way."

Claire breathed a sigh of relief that she hadn't been shut down—but only seconds later, she asked, "Well, what about avenging the death of your mother? Wouldn't she want you to find out what happened?"

"Maybe," Hilda replied. "I don't know. She wasn't a very curious or judgmental person. She just believed in *live and let live*." But Claire heard a sob on the phone.

"Look, Hilda. May I just come over again so we can talk about this a bit more? I promise not to push."

"Uh. Oh—okay, I guess."

"I'll be right over. What's your favorite drink from Starbucks? I'll bring it."

Twenty minutes later, Claire was there with two Venti-sized Pumpkin Chai Lattes. *Having the same drink will increase our sense of solidarity*, Claire thought. But that wasn't the only reason that Claire had forsaken her usual plain black coffee. She'd been curious about trying this drink for a long time but had never wanted to spend the money. Now she could feel justified.

"I think they're still hot," she said by way of greeting when Hilda let her in. They sat in the family room this time and Roxie looked suspiciously from the doorway but didn't come in. Job took his usual post beside Hilda and looked with interest at their coffees. Claire wished she'd thought to bring him a treat to get in his good books. She wasn't good with animals, never having had a pet of her own.

"I checked Gary's emails," Hilda said abruptly. "There's nothing odd there."

"That's not surprising," Claire said evenly. "If somebody really was threatening him, they wouldn't want to do it in a way that anybody else could find out about. A better bet would be to see if he has any incriminating files on his computer. Maybe he came across something funny in his accounting work and the client found out."

"I never thought he was totally honest," Hilda said, thoughtfully. She sat back for a minute thinking, and then added, "I don't think my father was, either. The two of them liked each other and seemed to have an affinity. My mother was kind of on the outside of that. I think there were things going on that she didn't want to know about. I never thought of that as a child growing up but I can see it now. I knew Gary since I was thirteen. He was the son of one of my father's best clients. And when I got older it seemed like my father was always trying to push us together. But when I was nineteen, I met someone else, a so-called 'business man' named Albert LeSore and married him. That turned out to be a disaster and I later got a divorce. He was very happy when I later decided to marry Gary—or Tom, as he was called then. I remember that."

After a pause, Claire said, "Don't you think your mother cared where the money came from? She never struck me as that kind of person."

"Oh, I think, looking back, that she cared. She just felt helpless to do anything about it but I remember the worried expression of her face at times. She wasn't like that herself but she was kind of passive. She never worked outside the home or had any ambition to work. I think she just thought she'd made her bed and had to lie in it. I could see that my father was kind of contemptuous of her in some ways and I'm afraid I got that way, too. I just thought she wasn't very smart or very strong." Hilda put her head down then and Claire saw the tears silently falling.

A few minutes passed and Claire said nothing. She didn't know what to say and wondered if Hilda would want her to leave now. She wondered what Tia would do in this situation. Finally, Hilda took a sip of her latte and looked at her.

"I guess you feel guilty now," Claire blurted. "Guilt is a terrible thing! It makes you forget about anything good you've ever done and just feel like a rotten, horrible person." Claire was speaking from her own experience, recalling several things she'd done in her life that she fervently wished she'd done differently.

Hilda looked at her surprised. "Everybody sees you as a paragon of virtue, Claire. What could you have done that's so awful?"

"I guess we all have things we're not proud of but we don't usually want to let others know." As Claire said this, she was registering how many clichés Hilda used. That was something else they had in common!

"Well, what would you do now if you were in my position?" Hilda asked.

"I don't know," Claire said thoughtfully. "If something happened to Jessie or Dan I honestly don't know how I could cope. I'd remember every lie I ever told him so he wouldn't interfere with our murder investigations—and all the times I dumped Jessie on him when we didn't have any help. I love Jessie but I always resent having to do the work with her. I think she can feel it because she definitely relates better to Dan than to me."

"I guess you know how I feel then," Hilda said softly.

"In some ways but not in others. Dan and I are very close. And my mother died when I was very young and my stepmother didn't care about me at all. I think she always wished I wasn't there." Claire sensed that Hilda was thinking of her own mother then and how much Marion had loved her. She saw the glint of tears in Hilda's eyes.

"Fine, but what do I do?" Hilda demanded.

"Work!" Claire said with sudden energy. "Work is something we both understand. Let's work together to solve this murder. Because I'm convinced it was a murder. I remember that ramp. It doesn't make any sense for a car to come shooting out of there without stopping. Something else was going on. I'm sure of it!" The dog was whining softly at the door now and Claire said suddenly. "Let's take the dog for a walk and discuss an action plan."

Hilda said nothing but got up to get the dog's leash.

Chapter 15: The Team Gets Involved

It was the next evening and Gus, Amanda, Tia and Claire sat around Tia's kitchen table planning a strategy. Jimmy had taken Mario bowling, one of his continuing efforts to teach his overly serious and intellectual ten-year old adopted son how to have fun. Mario knew that this cause was very important to Jimmy so he went along with it although he could think of many ways he'd rather be spending his time— refining his computer programming skills, for example.

After Tia and Claire had shared with the others what they knew to date, Gus asked, "So where do we go from here?" Meanwhile, Amanda was typing furiously on her laptop. She took her job as group secretary very seriously and didn't want to miss recording any possibly relevant point.

"Hilda phoned me this afternoon and told me she'd been through Gary's client files and didn't see anything there that could have made someone angry enough to kill," Claire replied.

"Shouldn't we be the judges of that?" Gus asked. "We're the ones with experience solving murders!"

Claire hid a smile, always amused and often appalled at how seriously Gus took herself, and replied, "Actually, Hilda is concerned about client confidentiality."

"Then how are we supposed to help her?" Gus grumped.

"I have an idea," Amanda said thoughtfully. "I'm not convinced that we're going to find anything useful in those files either. But what if Gary had some hidden, compartmentalized files under a separate password that Hilda doesn't even know about?"

"Well, again, how do we look for them if we can't get access to the computer?" Gus asked impatiently.

"Matthew!" Amanda declared, with a cunning look on her face.

"Who's Matthew?" Tia and Claire asked together in surprise.

"Matthew is my 16-year-old grandson from Brandon, Manitoba. He got in trouble for hacking into the school computer system to find out why his coach didn't let him onto the football team this year and he was expelled. His parents are fed up with him and they're sending him here to complete his grade 12 year. He'll be living with us."

"Yeah, I'm thrilled," Gus said sarcastically. "He's going to be taking over the downstairs bedroom and that might interfere with Waldorf and Salatta using their favorite window sills in the rec room!" Amanda shook her head in disgust.

"Well," Tia asked. "If his parents are sending him here for a fresh start and presumably to keep him out of trouble, how are they going to feel about you asking him to crack into hidden files on a computer? That's what you're getting at, isn't it?"

"What they don't know won't hurt them," Amanda muttered.

"Wa-a-it a minute!" Claire exclaimed. "I thought you said you never married?"

"I didn't," Amanda replied. "When I was sixteen, I fell madly in love with a senior in my high school. I got pregnant and my parents shipped me off to live with an aunt for that school year. They insisted that I give the baby away. When my son, Olaf, was 21, he contacted me. Apparently, he'd been searching for some time and the law had changed by that time so the clerk at the birth registry was obliged to give him my name and what information they had. Then he went through the marriage registry and found me. He grew up in Manitoba with a Scandinavian couple, last name of Gustafson. I never saw much of him through the years but when he married and had a son, Olaf asked if the three of them could visit me. After that, I visited them periodically, and Matthew and I somehow ended up forming a closer connection than I ever had with his father and now he wants to come here to finish his high school. It was that or a boarding school and he chose me." Amanda said this last in an understated way but there was a note of pride in her voice.

After several minutes of conversation and congratulation from Tia and Claire over this interesting turn of events, while Gus continued to scowl, the talk returned to the problem at hand. "Whether or not there are hidden files, and whether or not Matthew can access them is all academic anyway since Hilda doesn't want to hand over the computer," Claire reminded them.

"I think I have a solution for that," Amanda said. "You tell her to pull the confidential files off on a memory stick and then delete them from the hard drive. Then let us have the computer long enough to check for any hidden files. I'll put Matthew to work on it and if he finds anything that might relate to a client file, I'm sure he'll know how to recover the deleted files. It's really hard to permanently delete files from a computer."

"But like you said, if there are hidden files they're probably password protected. How are we ever going to figure out his password before the magic three tries when the computer locks you out?"

"Psychology, Claire! I'm going to spend some time visiting with Hilda and learning about Gary—what he liked and was interested in and what he didn't like. Most people choose passwords with personal meaning to them so they can remember them more easily."

"When is Matthew getting here?" Tia asked.

"He arrives tomorrow."

"But Hilda is certainly not going to want some sixteen-year-old mucking around with her husband's computer!"

"If you could get that computer just for a night, I could do a back-up and solve the whole problem!" Amanda muttered.

"I can see where Matthew gets his criminal tendencies!" Tia said drily. Gus snickered.

"I'll talk to Hilda again and see what she says. Meanwhile, let's move on to other possible directions our investigation can take," Claire suggested.

"I was thinking about the road," Amanda said, "and I pulled up an aerial map of the section you described on the computer. I think it would be worthwhile to go out there and closely examine the scene and try to recreate it in our minds. Maybe we could try coming down that ramp onto the highway at various speeds just to see how it feels."

"Hmm, I wonder how it would feel to get a ticket— or to have another accident?" Tia asked.

"Well, somehow we need to get a better understanding of how that accident could have happened," Amanda persisted.

"I agree," Claire said. "Why don't you and I take that on, Amanda?" Amanda nodded her head happily and Gus sniffed.

"I'll drive the van," Claire added. "Whoever hit them was driving a big van with a high center of gravity. Our van rides like that too and it's different taking the corners in it than it would be in Dan's little Toyota that hugs the road."

"Maybe you should take Jessie along on this trip, too—just in case she feels any vibes," Gus said sarcastically, referring to earlier occasions when Claire had had Jessie accompany her on potentially risky ventures because of her belief that Jessie was good at sensing when people had evil intentions.

Claire looked at her Aunt Gus but didn't reply directly. She knew where this mean remark was coming from. Gus was feeling hurt about being left out. "There's another avenue we could explore," Claire said thoughtfully. "Gary was an investment counselor in a mid-sized firm. How could we get one of his colleagues to talk to us about him?"

"Hmm," Gus said. "I do have a little money I could invest, and I could always pretend it was more. Maybe I could make an appointment to discuss it with someone and go back a couple of times for more information and gradually get to know him or her. Then I could casually raise the topic."

"That has possibilities!" Tia responded. "Why don't you take that on? I can ask Hilda what she knows about Gary's colleagues and which one she thinks it would be most useful to approach. Then you can pretend he or she was recommended to you by a friend."

Claire nodded her head in agreement. "Yes, it might lead to something—and we can't afford to pass up any possibility at this point."

"I'm going to call Sergeant Crombie and ask him what the possibilities are of getting an ID on the guy in the van," Tia said. "And, if possible, I think we should work more closely with him and Inspector McCoy this time around. I'm in no shape to do much snooping and you have a full-time job now, Claire." Tia turned to Gus, having picked up on Claire's signal, and explained, "I know you and Amanda can do a lot but I still think we're going to need extra help."

"But the police think it was an accident," Amanda pointed out.

"That's why I am going to start with Sergeant Crombie. He's the one most likely to listen when I tell him what we know so far."

The meeting ended at that point and they went their separate ways.

Chapter 16: Amanda gets Contact Information for Gus

At Gus' urging, Amanda met with Hilda the next day to ask her about the people in Gary's firm. She outlined their plan to have Gus go there claiming she wanted to invest money. Hilda was resistant at first, stating that she'd be more comfortable having Amanda do it. Amanda explained that they worked as a team and that was the team decision that had been made.

Amanda was a pleasant enough looking woman of average weight. However, she had a rather grim countenance and the rounded belly and sagging breasts that come to most women with age unless they fight vigorously against them. Her clothing was respectable but tended to be on the practical, easy care/easy wear side. And she had a no nonsense manner that didn't immediately attract people to her.

Gus, on the other hand, had launched a life-long battle against aging, her wardrobe of corsets being only one aspect of that. She had been blessed with *good bones,* a pleasant oval face, high cheekbones, well-spaced eyes, and a thin, straight Grecian nose. Her lips had been full in her youth and had not withered to the thin line so often seen in women her age. Where she had not been so fortunate was in the hair department, and in compensation she had a substantial collection of wigs, hairpieces and false eyelashes—different ones for different purposes.

Gus (she introduced herself as Augusta on important occasions) had always watched her weight rigidly and was on the thin side for someone her age. And her wardrobe was very impressive, which was probably why she actually had only a very modest amount of money to invest. But that fact didn't need to be disclosed immediately to the investment counselor and she could always say she'd changed her mind about investing before it came down to that. All in all, Gus' various attributes plus her regal bearing, a by-product of her vanity, made her the obvious choice for this part of the operation.

Amanda explained all this to Hilda and eventually Hilda agreed to share the necessary information. They discussed together the various people working at the firm and settled on two who'd known Gary quite well and had been to the house for social gatherings a couple of times on the rare occasions when Hilda and Gary entertained.

Sean Barich had actually attended the same MBA program as Gary and they had joined the firm about the same time, ten years ago or so. Hilda thought that if anybody knew what Gary was thinking or doing workwise these days it would be him. Dave Stout, on the other hand, had only come to the firm three years previously, but he and Gary shared a passion for racquetball and often went off to a neighborhood bar together after work for a drink. Sean usually did not join them, as he wanted to get home to his family as soon as possible.

"It sounds to me like Gus needs to find a reason to talk to both of them," Amanda said. "I hope she can pull it off."

"Well, I've been thinking about that," Hilda replied. When I feel more up to it, I think I'll hold memorial services for Gary and Marion, and I'm sure they'd both come." Hilda paused for a moment and then went on. "I'll have to collect the cremains first and choose urns for them, I suppose. Maybe I'll put Gary's ashes in a piggy bank since he was so focused on money!" Hilda added bitterly.

"I think saying good-bye is important," Amanda agreed, wincing inwardly at Hilda's bitterness. "But a memorial service would hardly be the place to talk to anyone about Gary's financial or personal affairs."

"Well, I guess you'll just have to do what you can then," Hilda conceded.

They left it at that. Although Amanda was itching to talk about the computer, she'd promised to wait until Tia found out more from Sergeant Crombie. Also, Matthew was arriving that afternoon and she wanted a chance to ask him certain questions so she'd know the best way to put Hilda's confidentiality fears at rest and get her hands on the computer. Amanda was hoping that she could meet again with Hilda tomorrow and convince her somehow to let her borrow it. She had a funny feeling that it was the key to their investigation and that accessing it as soon as possible was critical.

Chapter 17: Gus Prepares to Invest

Gus had been reviewing her wardrobe and making her plans, and once Amanda got the contact information for the people at the investment firm she was ready to go. After talking it over, Amanda suggested that the best person to approach first would be Sean Barich. If Gary really had been murdered, it likely had more to do with his professional work than his recreational activities. Gus just liked the sound of his name.

Gus phoned the receptionist at Gary's firm who identified herself as Janet Albright. Gus explained that a friend had recommended Sean and she would like to talk to him about investing.

"I'm available to meet on Monday, Wednesday or Friday mornings next week if any of those times work."

Gus was avoiding Tuesday and Thursday since she accompanied Claire's daughter, Jessie, to a grade-8 drama class on those afternoons. The receptionist offered an 11 a.m. appointment on Monday and, after hesitating briefly, Gus accepted.

It was now Friday, and Gus just hoped she'd be properly prepared by then. Fortunately, she'd been to the hair stylist only the week before to have her hair trimmed and dyed the soft honey blond tone she preferred. The eleven o'clock appointment time with Sean Barich on Monday meant she could get it professionally styled that morning if she could get an early enough appointment—and she was in luck.

Monday morning came all too soon and Gus woke with mixed feelings of apprehension and excitement.

She dressed quickly and left for her 7 o'clock hair appointment. Mercifully, coffee was on offer. Once back home, Gus (power dressing for the occasion, this time with the blessing of Amanda) put on her most unforgiving corset over which her new red wool suit, cut just below the knees, fit sleekly. A pewter grey, long-sleeved silk blouse with soft pleats in front but no ruffles, taupe-colored stockings to hide the few dark veins in her legs, and stylish, pale grey leather dress shoes with three inch heels completed the look— feminine but not fussy, powerful but not unapproachable.

When Gus arrived at the investment firm, Janet, the receptionist, sent her to the third floor where Sean's office was located.

Gus glanced at her self in the elevator mirror on the way up and was satisfied. She was so glad she'd been able to get her hair styled that morning. Otherwise, she'd have had to wear one of her wigs, and wigs could be very dangerous. A careless moment, a hand moved over them the wrong way, could allow them to end up askew, thus ruining the whole effect she was striving so hard to create.

Sean introduced himself and ushered her to a comfortable chair. He took the one opposite with a small round table in between them. Gus crossed her legs and looked at him with as pleasant an expression on her face as she could manage, given how nervous she was. "Now, what can I do for you, Mrs.—er, Miss Kalline?"

"It's Ms.," she replied somewhat coolly. *Let him think I'm a glamorous divorcee,* she thought. *He's likely to take me more seriously than if he thinks I'm either a widow or a spinster.* Actually, Kalline was her married name, but her husband had died 23 years earlier of pancreatic cancer. He'd never been much of a go-getter and it had been her income that primarily supported them. She had not been particularly sorry when he died.

Out loud, Gus said, "I have some money to invest. We're talking only 50 to 100 thou, nothing big. I'd just like to try you out on a small scale. I haven't been entirely satisfied with the returns on the portfolios I'm holding with Manulife."

Gus could see that she had his interest and he began pulling out various charts and telling her what he thought would be the most profitable way to invest her money. He discussed the annual returns of various portfolios averaged over the past five and ten years. He suggested that since she was a senior, she should stick to low to medium-low risk investments. Otherwise, she might not have enough time to regain her capital if there was a sudden market slump.

Gus sniffed audibly at this reference to her age and Sean backtracked quickly. "Actually, when I met you just now I took you to be in your 50's but since you told our receptionist that you were retired, I was thinking I must be wrong. Please excuse me."

Gus looked somewhat appeased by this statement and didn't bother to correct him. But she also didn't know what else to say. What she'd told him to date about her investment plans had been carefully rehearsed with Amanda who was far more money smart than Gus. Gus preferred to spend money to maintain her image rather than to invest it for some distant return.

Since Gus had no idea how to respond intelligently when Sean asked her which portfolio interested her, she did the only thing she could do—pasted a skeptical look on her face and silently willed him to explain more. But just then there was a knock on the door. Gus saw a quick look of irritation cross his features before they smoothed out again and he excused himself to respond.

Always curious, Gus leaned over in her chair to peep around Sean's shoulder in order to see who'd been so rude as to interrupt them. She was sure the receptionist would've told the person that Sean was occupied. A tall man, older but fit looking, stood in the doorway and their eyes met—and held.

"Gustava?"

"Johnny?"

Chapter 18: Echoes from the Past

John Barich crossed the room towards Gus and she rose in a daze from her chair and walked right into his open arms. They just stood there like that and, since no introductions seemed forthcoming, Sean finally crossed the floor behind them, plucked his suit jacket off his desk chair, picked up two files and his laptop from his desk and said, "If either of you wants me, I'll be in your office, Dad." He left then, closing the door softly behind him, and a huge grin lit up his face once he was safely outside. "So that's the Gustava Lind Dad mentions so casually as "an old girlfriend." I can't wait to tell my sisters!"

John and Gus settled in Sean's two comfortable office chairs and, by unspoken agreement, prepared to catch up on the 40 years that had passed since they last saw each other.

"Why did you leave?" he asked. "I never understood."

"It was crazy," Gus replied. I was five years older than you. That might work today but not in those days. People would have talked."

"You always cared too much about what people think."

"Yes," she conceded, "and I paid a high price for it."

"We paid a high price for it!"

"What do you mean? That was your son I was talking to, wasn't it? So you must have married and had a family. That's more than I had."

"Yes, I married. I was married for 35 years until my wife died three years ago of stomach cancer. Sean is my oldest and I have two daughters, Sadie and Rebecca. They all live here in the city so I haven't been too lonely. They look after me well."

"Do you miss your wife very much?"

"Yes, in some ways. We had a good, solid relationship. We always supported each other and looked out for each other." John paused for a minute and then added, "But I never forgot you, Gustava."

"Nobody calls me that anymore. In fact, I go by Augusta now—but most people just call me Gus."

"Why did you change your name?"

"I don't know. I think Augusta suits me better—suits the person I have become."

"And who is that person? What have you been doing with your life since last I saw you?"

Gus put her head down. She didn't want him to know that she'd frittered away large chunks of it worrying about appearance and carving out small forms of one-upmanship. But she also didn't feel like lying to someone who'd been so important to her.

"I finished that degree in Theatre Arts I was working on part-time when you knew me and I worked away at my music until I completed grade 10 in piano at the conservatory. But that didn't lead to a job so I went to business school and became a secretary. In the later years of my career I became an office manager for a small company specializing in temp replacements for office work."

"What about men?"

"I was almost 40 when I finally married and Geoff was close to 50. He had a middle management position at a department store but a few years later, he was declared redundant and laid off. He couldn't seem to get another job and then he got pancreatic cancer. He died 23 years ago."

John started to express condolences but Gus cut him off. "I felt sorry for him but I don't think I ever really loved him. He never did measure up to you, Johnny," she said wistfully.

Much more was said between them and another hour passed before there was a tentative knock on the door. Sean opened it a crack and called out, "Dad, may I come in? I need to get some files."

Gus stood up and hastily gathered her purse and her jacket which had been removed somewhere along the way. "I better be going. Amanda will be wondering where I am."

"Did you drive?" John asked.

"No. I took a cab."

"Then let me drive you home, please. I'd love to meet your cats. We had a wonderful cat, Gladiator, for 16 years—but he died recently. I miss him."

Chapter 19: John Meets Amanda. Gus Blurts. Amanda Cringes

Amanda saw the sleek grey Mercedes drive up and gawked in amazement as Gus stepped daintily out of it, the door held open for her by a distinguished-looking older man. Moments later, they were in the house and Gus introduced Amanda to John, explaining that he was "an old friend" she hadn't seen for many years. They sat in the living room together, drinking coffee and eating Amanda's health-infused pecan crunch cookies, her culinary specialty. The talk turned to their current activities.

"You'll need to make another appointment with Sean to sort our your investment plans, Gustava," John said. You're going to be very happy with his advice. He has an excellent track record!"

"Gustava? Who are you talking about?" exclaimed Amanda. Explanations followed with Gus looking shamefaced and John remorseful.

To change the subject, Gus started talking about the detective work she and her friends had become involved in over the past three years. "Currently, we're looking into Gary's death."

"But that was an accident! That's what I heard on the news."

"We're not so sure. From a couple of things we've found out, we suspect it might have been murder—and that it was likely due to something he uncovered at work." Amanda glared at Gus and for a fleeting moment a guarded expression came over John's face. Gus realized what she'd done and looked stricken.

John saw the look and said softly, "No, Gussie. It wasn't me. I thought for a moment about Sean but he's always been very upright in his business dealings. I'm sure it wasn't him either."

"Well, you *would* say that, wouldn't you?" Amanda stated.

An uncomfortable silence filled the room and Gus thought frantically of something else to say. Finally, she blurted out in an unnaturally cheery tone, "John, you said you wanted to meet my cats. They're downstairs in my private sitting room."

"I'd like that, Gus," he replied, rising from his chair. John turned to Amanda and thanked her for her hospitality, making it clear that their visit was over. Then the two of them retired to the basement.

Once they were alone, John grabbed her. "Gus, I swear to you that if something is going on at the company it has nothing to do with me—and I'm positive it has nothing to do with Sean either. But we can help you. I can tell you, for example, that there was a surprise audit at the firm last year and apparently some irregularities were uncovered. I don't know more than that because I'm only there a few hours a week these days, just to look after two or three clients who aren't yet ready to switch over to a different investment counselor so I can fully retire." After a pause, he added thoughtfully, "But Sean might know. He did mention to me once that he thought some insider trading might be going on."

Gus sat down abruptly, overwhelmed by the entire situation. She didn't know what to say or do. All she knew was it felt like her whole world had tilted and the last thing she wanted was to push this man back out of her life a second time.

They looked at each other and suddenly he jerked her back to her feet and pinned her tightly with his arms. "Gus! Gus, I don't want to lose you a second time. I...." Whatever he'd planned to say was lost as his lips touched hers and suddenly they were both caught up in a kiss so deep and long that it spanned all the years between them.

John moaned and his hand went beneath her jacket to clasp her breast. But a wall of resistance met him. "What's this?" he asked, surprised.

"I had to look the part," Gus said defensively.

"What part was that?"

"You know, kind of sexy and powerful. How else was I going to get Sean to tell me anything?"

John grinned. "Well, I can tell you that wouldn't have worked on him anyway. He's a very strong family man!"

"And I'm a foolish old woman!" Gus said ruefully.

"No. You're a beautiful, smart, sexy old woman," he replied, fumbling around beneath her jacket.

"What are you doing?"

"I don't think we have time for a long courtship," he replied. But before he could argue further there was a sharp knock at the door.

Chapter 20: Emergency

When Gus answered the door, she found Amanda there looking very upset.

"What happened?"

"Hilda just called. She said she'd gone to the corner store to get some milk, and in those few minutes someone broke in. Her dog tried to stop him but the thief shot him. Hilda's on her way to the vet with him right now."

"What did he take?" Gus asked.

"Apparently, he was just after Gary's computer. The mailman came to the door just as the thief opened it to leave and the thief was so startled that he dropped the computer in the flowerbed and ran off. Maybe he mistook him for a policeman. Their uniforms are quite similar.

"Did Hilda call the police?"

"No—but she asked me to go to her house and get the—*damn*— computer. She said she doesn't care about confidentiality any more and just to get my grandson to take a look at it. She told me where the spare key is."

John had been listening to all this and he said, "I'll drive you. Then we'll go to the vet, if you know which one it is, and check on Hilda and the dog. She'll need support."

Amanda turned to him suspiciously. "You excused yourself earlier when we were talking and made a phone call. Who did you call?"

He pulled out his phone and dialed a number and put the phone on speaker. "Sheridan Investments!" a voice sang over the phone.

"Hi, Janet. It's John. What time did I phone you last?"

"Uh, just after one? I just got back from my lunch break." Clearly she was confused.

John didn't explain, but instead asked, "And what did I call you about?"

"To cancel your two o'clock appointment?"

"Thank you, Janet. I'll explain some day. Bye." John turned around and looked at them. "Satisfied?"

"You could have made a second call," Amanda argued.

"He's not like that!" Gus said angrily. "And anyway, he was only gone a couple of minutes. It would take longer than that to explain why he needed the computer grabbed, if that's what you're thinking."

John looked at her gratefully and then said, "Let's go! We're wasting time!"

They piled into the Mercedes and took off. Collecting the computer was straightforward and soon they were on their way to the vet, Amanda having phoned Hilda back to get the address.

"How is he?" Amanda asked, when they entered the building and saw Hilda sitting tensely in the waiting room.

"He was shot in the foreleg," Hilda said with a sob. "They think they may have to remove it!"

"Let me talk to them!" John said.

Hilda looked at him suspiciously. There had been no time for introductions. But Gus nodded her head and Hilda agreed.

John was gone a long time but when he returned he assured Hilda that Job could keep his leg. "It's quite a delicate operation, but I signed a paper saying I'd cover the bill. Apparently, they don't normally even offer it as an option because most people won't consider it, given the cost."

"But why are you doing this?" Hilda asked, amazed. "I don't even know you!"

"I like animals—and I like Gus. Any friend of Gustava is a friend of mine!"

Hilda looked surprised at the name but said nothing about it. After thanking him copiously for his generosity, she asked, "Did you get the computer?"

"Yes!" Amanda said "And I need to get back to the house. Matthew will be arriving within the hour!"

"I'll be fine now," Hilda said. "Just go. And find those bastards who're doing all this!"

"We will!" Gus said with some of her old hutzpah. "We always do!"

Chapter 21: Matthew Arrives and Gus Leaves

When they returned to Amanda's house, they found Matthew waiting patiently on the porch. Amanda looked anxious and apologetic. It was January in Edmonton, after all. But the young man assured her that he'd only arrived a few minutes earlier. Introductions were made with Gus greeting him coolly and John formally. Gus and John quickly retired to Gus' sitting room, leaving Amanda to settle Matthew into his room, describe the 'accident' and the break-in, and show him the computer.

Once they were alone, John turned to her. "Gus, there's something I want to ask you. I have a seven-day Caribbean cruise booked for a week from tomorrow, leaving from Miami. I chose a luxury cabin for two because I like a little space, but I'm travelling alone. I'm pretty sure there are still first-class plane tickets available and I'd like you to go with me."

"Oh, no, Johnny. I couldn't. It wouldn't look … I have responsibilities … I need to work on my part of this investigation, find out what was happening at Gary's workplace, if anything, that could have led to his death."

"Now that I've found you again I don't want to be separated from you. I can't risk losing you a second time," he argued.

"I'll be here when you get back," she said. I accompany my grandniece, Jessica, twice a week to a grade-8 drama class and I must continue working on the investigation. Look what happened at Hilda's house today!"

"Fine! I just have two appointments this week and I'll spend the rest of my time helping you with this investigation. Meanwhile, can you find somebody to take over in the drama class for the week we would be gone? I'm going to order that extra plane ticket. If we have this wrapped up by then—or your part in it anyway—will you come?"

Gus looked at him. She didn't know what to say— but then she remembered all the lonely years and all the wasted time. "Okay." *What have I done?* she asked herself. But somehow she knew it was the right thing.

"Good!" he replied. "Now I'm going to phone Sean and ask him to meet us at my condo at seven for dinner. We'll find out what he knows then. Pack a bag so you can stay over. We will likely be running late!" Gus looked at him. "Would you rather stay here with Matthew?" He'd witnessed her response to him. "And do you really think we should waste any more time?"

"Uh, I might need to stop at the store. I believe all my night clothes are in the wash." Gus was thinking of the comfy but highly unflattering granny nightgowns stacked neatly in her dresser drawer.

"Don't worry. I'll keep you warm!" he said cheerfully. And, as I recall, you never used to worry so much about nightgowns!" Gus blushed.

"I'll pack," she said. "But I may not stay—and I'm assuming you have a second bedroom? And before we go, I want us to stop by Claire's house so you can meet her and Jessie—and Dan," she added grudgingly as an afterthought. "But particularly Jessie."

"No problem—and yes I have a second bedroom. Although I'm hoping you won't use it." John picked up the phone and walked out into the hall to call Sean and his housekeeper. Sean agreed to the meeting and the housekeeper assured him she'd have a decent meal for the three of them on the table at seven and take care of his other requests as well.

Meanwhile, Gus was nervously packing. After rummaging through drawers and closets, she finally found a long black silk slip to wear in bed, just in case. It at least looked more youthful and appealing than her flannel nightgowns!

Claire was predictably surprised to see them and shocked to find out who John was. He talked to Jessie for a bit and she bestowed one of her special smiles on him. Gus finally realized that this was what she'd been looking for—Jessie's approval. She suddenly felt lighter.

Over a glass of wine, they explained to Claire a little of their story and told her of their plans to meet with Sean that evening to see what they could learn about Gary's recent business dealings. Dan came in from work then and introductions were made and explanations given. "I hope you know what you're getting into, man," he commented jokingly to John, but with an undercurrent of meaning.

"I know exactly who Gustava is and I've always loved her for it," he replied, with just a little bit of steel in his voice. Gus relished the moment, an extra score for her in her ongoing rivalry with Dan!

It's unfathomable that somebody as vain and self-centered as Gus could attract a guy like that, Dan thought. But when he saw the glow on her face and the light in John's eyes, his heart softened. Maybe Claire's right to be annoyed with me over my uncharitable attitude. Jessie likes her, after all. And that has to count for something.

Chapter 22: Adventures in the Condo

Gus and John left soon after and headed for John's condo on Saskatchewan Drive near the University of Alberta. As they approached, Gus was mentally calculating how she'd get to Jessie's school the next day so she could accompany her to her drama class. She could take a bus to the university, then the LRT (light rail transit) to Southgate and then get another bus from there to go the short distance to Jessie's school, or maybe a taxi for that part if necessary.

Because of this inner monologue, Gus was not paying much attention to the building itself and when they entered John's unit, she gasped in surprise. His condo was on the sixth floor and a wall of windows provided a spectacular view of the North Saskatchewan River and Edmonton's downtown skyline. Soft leather chairs and sofas in a smoky gray, and elegant teak pieces, more traditional than some of their contemporary counterparts, graced the spacious living room. One wall was largely taken up by a massive book shelf overflowing with interesting looking books. Several intriguing paintings occupied the remaining wall space. But she'd need to examine them later because just then a middle-aged woman of indefinable background emerged from what Gus assumed was the kitchen area.

John introduced Gus to his housekeeper, Betty Medeas, and just then Sean arrived. Between the knowing look that Betty gave her and Sean's stoically neutral gaze, Gus felt quite rattled. However, a gin and tonic soon revived her and loosened her tongue and she began to tell both men all she knew about Gary's death.

In the middle of this recital, Gus' phone rang. It was Tia, who started to tell her she'd spoken to Sergeant Crombie and he'd shared something very interesting. Gus immediately perked up, put the phone on speaker and motioned to the men to pay attention. "What Inspector Crombie told me," Tia said, "is that forensics identified the remains of a crash helmet on the head of the guy who died in the van. All the plastic had melted but they found the wires around his head and they're pretty sure that's what it was."

"That's very interesting," Gus said slowly. "I'm with Sean and his father right now and I'll discuss this with them. I've…"

Tia interrupted at that point to say, "Yes, I've heard about the father. Hubba, hubba!"

Gus abruptly shut off the speaker button, blushing furiously. "As I was about to say, Tia, before you interrupted, I'd already put the phone on speaker!"

"Oops!" Tia responded. "My bad. Sorry!" But she didn't sound sorry and, even without the benefit of the speaker, she'd heard the sound of snickering in the background.

Gus hung up the phone and looked at the two men who were struggling hard to keep their faces straight. "We need to focus here!" she said, more harshly than she intended. "Gary drove a small, two-door sports car. A large van driven by a man wearing a crash helmet hit his car broadside from the right, connecting directly with the passenger door. According to what the two police officers told Hilda, there were no skid marks to suggest that the van slowed down at all before impact. In fact, the tracks indicated that instead of entering the highway at the end of the merge lane it was driven straight across the grass and aimed directly at Gary's car.

"Maybe the steering and brakes failed?" Sean offered.

"No. There was no identifiable evidence of mechanical failure in either car. There was some indication of wear on the brake linings in Gary's car but Hilda says he had a tendency to ride the brakes. The van that hit them was in perfect mechanical condition as far as could be determined after the fire damage."

"You said earlier that Gary's car exploded on impact because of the faulty fuel line but did the van explode too?" John asked.

"I don't know. But from what I've heard it was completely engulfed in flames the same as Gary's car. There was no way the driver could get out." Gus turned to Sean and explained, "You see, a tanker truck was passing them in the left-hand lane so Gary's car was sandwiched between the two. That's why the impact was so severe."

"The driver of the van must have thought he could get away?" Sean asked.

"Yes, but he couldn't have anticipated a tanker truck passing a sports car! That must have happened because Gary was driving so slowly, as several witnesses reported."

"Do the police have any idea why?" John asked.

"They did find the remains of a cell phone on the floor of the car so he obviously had it out. Maybe he was talking to somebody." Gary's car had been recalled because of the danger of fuel line rupture upon impact but he wasn't yet aware of the recall. It's unlikely the man who hit him could have known about that recall so he couldn't have anticipated that there would be a fire and he himself would be in danger. What does all this tell us?"

"Somebody set out to kill Gary thinking that by wearing a crash helmet and driving a much bigger and heavier vehicle, he'd be quite safe hitting a car half his size?" Sean offered. "The fire and the tanker were unanticipated. By the way, did the tanker catch fire and explode?"

"No. Apparently it was carrying milk. But that's why the firemen didn't get the bodies out sooner. They didn't know that and were afraid to go near it in case it exploded. Anyway, I think there's enough evidence to suggest this was more than an accident. Do you agree, Johnny?" Sean stifled a snicker at her use of the pet name.

John didn't respond directly but asked instead, "With the break-in at Hilda's and the evidence of the crash helmet, are the police going to start treating this as a murder?"

"Apparently. And the first thing they're going to do is to come after Gary's computer so I hope that Matthew kid was able to get something," Gus replied. "I should phone Amanda and see what's happening."

"They probably know already so why bother right now. Eat your dinner," John argued.

"It's too important to risk. For all I know that kid is just goofing around instead of working on it." Gus picked up the phone and made the call. John would learn that he would not get very far telling Gus what to do.

As it happened, Hilda had called Amanda immediately when she found out about the helmet and Matthew had been working furiously at trying to crack the password ever since. Sean and John were listening to Gus' half of the call and at this point Sean held up his finger to interrupt. Gus put the phone on speaker and asked Amanda to do so as well.

"Gary used to gripe to me about Marion a lot. He often made fun of her, too, and of her tendency to repeat the same stories. 'I came from Paisley in 66. I came from Paisley in 66' he would mimic in a high falsetto." They heard Matthew's voice in the background saying, "Paisley66. That would make a perfect password!" He quickly typed it in and the page opened. He and Amanda both shouted gleefully.

Gus interrupted their happy moment and anxiously said, "Make copies of everything, Amanda, as quick as you can. The police could come to the door to collect the computer at any time!"

"It'll all be on a memory stick in a minute and then, if I have time, I'll do a complete back-up," Matthew replied with a slight sneer in his voice—but not so slight that Gus did not pick up on it.

"Fine!" she said huffily, and hung up the phone.

"Well, that's one problem solved," John commented.

"Yes, but we need more," Gus replied. "Sean, is there anything unusual about the way Gary had been acting recently? Has he had any strange phone calls or messages that you know of?"

"I think my father already told you that we had a forensic audit last year. It upset everybody! Gary talked about it for days and seemed quite nervous. But apart from that, he didn't confide in me and if anything funny was going on I don't know about it," Sean replied.

Gus thanked him for his input, especially for the help with the password. It was doubtful that they could have cracked it otherwise. But soon after dinner, having received a silent message from his father, Sean said his good-byes, claiming the need to get home to his family.

Chapter 23: The Moment of Truth

The housekeeper cleared the last of the dishes and declared that she was going home. After she left, John took Gus by the hand and led her towards his bedroom. She resisted, presenting all sorts of reasons why she really should return home or at least sleep in the other bedroom. He ignored them and led her directly into his spacious ensuite bathroom where the generously-sized hot tub was full of warm, scented water. Fluffy towels and pristine white dressing gowns had been laid out on a warming rack nearby. Gus took one look and turned to leave.

"I can't do this, John. It's way too soon. I really think I need to go home."

"I was afraid you were going to say that," John replied. "Won't you at least give me a chance to change your mind?" And with that he grabbed Gus and kissed her soundly, bending her further and further over the tub. She finally fell in, her feet still draped over the edge. John very considerately removed her shoes before assisting the rest of her in.

Gus shouted in outrage but John only said, "I'm sorry. I couldn't think of any other way to keep you here and I just couldn't let you go." He sat down on the rim of the tub beside her.

Fortunately, Gus had removed her suit jacket before dinner so as not to risk getting food on it. "I just hope this blouse doesn't shrink," she said grumpily. "It won't be easy to replace."

"I better help you to get it off as soon as possible, then," he said, leaning over and beginning to carefully undo the row of tiny buttons. Gus was basically speechless at this point. She didn't know what to say or do so she did nothing. John tossed her blouse gently onto the floor and then nudged her skirt off and tossed it to a different corner. "Just in case the dye runs. We wouldn't want it to stain that beautiful blouse. And if the skirt shrinks that's all to the good. It will just show more of your lovely legs!"

John then surveyed her with a look of befuddlement on his face. There was no doubt in his mind that Gus looked very enticing in the sexy black garment she was still wearing. He was later to learn that it was officially known as a 'steel-boned deep plunge satin corset.' But all he could think at that moment was that it looked virtually impossible to remove for anyone without the necessary skill set! An awkward silence prevailed and finally Gus said, "It has covered hooks in the front."

With fumbling fingers, John got to work. "If I ever manage to get this off I'm never going to let you put it back on again!" he said in exasperation. Finally, his efforts were rewarded and he tossed the offending corset into the furthest corner of the room.

He looked down at her legs then and slowly and gently began removing the silky taupe panty hose. Gus braced herself because he'd soon be seeing the small dark veins on her thighs and calves that she considered so ugly. But when the veins were revealed John just looked at them soberly and then softly kissed each one in turn. Gus felt the last of her resistance melting and John, sensing this, quickly stripped off his own clothes and joined her in the water.

Later, much later, John helped Gus out of the tub. They both moved creakily and he said, "Perhaps such acrobatics are best left to the young!" Gus looked at him and demurred. "I don't know," she said. "Sex has certainly improved since the last time I tried it. I guess you have to have a little pain for a little gain!"

John looked at her in surprise and appreciation. She was not the rigid, prudish girl he remembered. He wrapped one of the warm towels around her and held her close for a moment. Then he dried himself and they both put on the robes and toddled off to bed. But, stiff and tired as they were, the night was not uneventful.

Chapter 24: The Morning After

Gus woke suddenly, looking around in surprise at the strange room. She glanced over at John, snoring softly beside her. And then she wept. She wept not for what she'd done the night before but what she'd done 40 years ago and for all the years with him that had been lost forever because of it. John woke then and reached for her. Then they made love once again.

This was not the slow, tentative love of the night before but a rapid, hungry, almost violent kind of love. Soon a glorious humming sound filled her ears and waves of sensation rushed over her. "Oh, Gussie!" he called—and she heard another voice as well. "Johnny! My Johnny." She later realized it had been her own.

After, they lay back in bed just holding hands and staring at the ceiling. Several minutes passed and then Gus said one word, "Mouthwash."

"Mouthwash?"

"Yes. Mouthwash would make it perfect."

"Or else we could just not kiss in the morning."

"No, I don't like that idea."

"I know! I could install twin fountains on each side of the bed with shelves beside them for our own separate bottles of mouthwash. Then we could just gargle before we make love. Oh, wait," John went on. "Gargling isn't very romantic either."

Gus giggled then and wrapped her arms around him. "Do you think this is what they call a first world problem?"

John didn't respond directly, but said instead, "I hear the housekeeper preparing breakfast so you better get dressed. But not with that contraption! I forbid it."

Gus looked woefully at her skirt and blouse. She'd managed to rinse them and hang them up before going to bed but they badly needed pressing. And she wasn't even sure they'd fit anymore.

John read her thoughts and said, "I took the liberty of sending the housekeeper out to buy a few things for you yesterday. I checked the size of your jacket when you took it off at the office. I hope they fit and they are to your taste. He went to the closet and pulled out two full shopping bags from Holt Renfrew, a higher end Edmonton store where Gus rarely dared to shop.

Gus checked through the bags and found everything she would need, even a brassiere. This was vital since the corset was now off limits. She put on a lounge suit marketed as casual wear, but it was actually elegant enough to wear to Jessie's class. The brassiere worked but not perfectly—and she looked with some displeasure at the slight droop of her breasts that would not have been there with the corset. She also was not too happy about the rounding of her stomach that the corset was so good at suppressing. But finally she was ready for breakfast after putting on a minimum of make-up and donning one of the trusty wigs she'd brought with her.

John looked at her approvingly but frowned when he saw the wig. "What's wrong with your own hair? There's still one of my wife's curling irons around here somewhere if that's what you need."

"My hair needs more help than that—and the wig is not negotiable," Gus said a bit snappily.

"Okay," he replied, "if that's what it takes to make you comfortable. But you can see you don't need the corset. You look perfectly fine without it."

Gus looked down at her sagging breasts and bulging stomach. She glanced over her shoulder at the full-length mirror on the closet door and saw that her behind was drooping as well. "I wonder if you would have fallen back in love with me so rapidly if this is how I had looked yesterday!"

"We'll never know now," he said cheerily. "Suffice it to say that since falling back in love with you has already happened, the lack of a corset can't make it un-happen. So you have nothing to fear in that regard—unless you're still interested in attracting other men."

"Are you saying I'm not attractive to other men now?" Gus asked sharply.

"Oh, boy, John," he muttered to himself. "Learn to quit while you're ahead!" Speaking in a more normal tone, he said, "Breakfast is ready. We better get out there."

Betty wished them good-morning and asked if they'd slept well. Gus blushed and then agreed. "Thank you for getting the clothes, Betty. They fit well and I like them." She did not mention the unpadded, unwired, overly-relaxed brassiere that wouldn't hold her at an upright angle no matter how tightly she adjusted the straps.

As Betty was serving them, John mentioned casually, "By the way, Gustava, I thought we could go downtown to pick up the marriage license this morning before I drive you to the school so you can help your grandniece in her drama class. At some point I need to call my lawyer, too, about the pre-nup."

Gus just stared at him, not knowing, at first, what to say. But she understood intuitively why he'd chosen to mention these issues now. She knew he valued Betty and did not want to lose her. And clearly he wanted her to think well of Gus and not assume she was just a fling. Still, it put her in a difficult position. "Don't you think we're being a bit hasty?" she asked.

"No, I think 40 years is long enough and, as I said, I don't want us to lose out again the second time around!"

Gus noted that John had carefully avoided saying who had made the choice for them to "lose out" the first time. The male ego at work, she supposed. *Well, apart from that little detail, he certainly gave Betty enough information to form a positive view of me,* Gus thought, *so I should be grateful for that, anyway.*

"I guess it wouldn't hurt to go down there and check things out," she finally replied. "The process might be more complicated than you remember."

Chapter 25: The Pre-Nup

They argued all the way downtown but in the end John won. The marriage license was procured and a date chosen during the cruise when they'd be docking overnight in Barbados. He graciously allowed Gus to choose that detail. "Claire and Tia have been there," she explained, "and I've always wondered what it was like. Besides, I like the fact that it is—or was—an English colony!"

"Do you have a thing for the English?" he asked.

"A bit," Gus acknowledged. "Why? You don't share my feelings?"

"I've always found them a little on the snobby side."

"Maybe you're a little on the snobby side—and that's why you clash!" she retorted, her old tendency towards irritability rearing its ugly head. He looked at her, surprised by her tone, and Gus immediately apologized.

"I guess I'm just feeling overwhelmed by everything," she said, in an effort to excuse herself.

"In a happy way, I hope?" he asked guardedly.

"Yes, Johnny," Gus said, sighing. "In fact, I can't remember when I've been so happy."

"I'm glad," he said, grasping her hand.

They were on their way to the school so Gus could accompany Jessie to the drama class. "Otherwise," as she'd explained to him, "she can't go—and she really likes it!"

"There's something else I need to discuss with you, Gussie, and I hope it won't damage your happy mood. I

phoned my lawyer this morning while you were getting
ready and made an appointment with him to draw up a
pre-nup." He looked at her cautiously out of the corner
of his eye.

"Good! Because I'm not going to marry you
otherwise!"

"What kind of settlement would you be expecting if
something happened to me or to us, then?" he asked.

"Settlement? Nothing! I looked after myself before
you came along and I'm sure I could do it again if you
died before me." Gus might be mean with her own
money but she had a strong sense of fairness and was
not about to start grasping after somebody else's.
"What you have should go to your children. That's only
right—and I'm sure that's how your late wife would
want it. Did you forget to think about her?"

John pulled the car off the road into a side lane and
parked. *I should not have attempted to have this
conversation while driving*, he thought. Fortunately,
they'd left for the school early and could afford to sit
there for 15 minutes or a little more if necessary. "You
know, Gussie," he said, "I know exactly what you mean
about feeling overwhelmed. I want to know all about
you as of yesterday—and I want all of you, all the
time!" He groaned and pulled her towards him,
clutching at her breast through the thin fabric of her
brassiere.

"John!" she exclaimed, obviously shocked. "Please!
We're in a public place!"

"Oh, yes," he sighed, and sat back sedately behind
the wheel. After a few moments, he resumed the former
conversation. "I've been thinking of my wife and
children. Before she died, Annie told me that she didn't
want me to be lonely. She said if I should find
somebody good and kind to marry who'd look after me,
well, I should do so, and I should look after her, too."

After a pause, he added naughtily, "She didn't mention sexy but I'm hoping she wouldn't mind that either— and since she isn't around to ask we'll just have to go on that assumption. Satisfied?"

Gus grinned and John went on. "If I die before you, I'm going to make sure you have enough money to live on nicely, as well as the house and all our joint possessions except for the few items I'll be leaving to the children. I have enough money put away apart from that to leave all three of them with a fair sum."

"Oh!" she said in a small voice. "Well, I'd make sure your children had it back after I was gone. That's only fair!" After a pause, she added, "But what little I have I'm leaving to Jessie. I hope you don't mind."

"I wouldn't have it any other way," he said, looking at her tenderly. "And whatever I leave you, if I go first, is yours to leave to whomever you want. My children would not resent that or even expect you to do otherwise. Now we'd better get going—because if we stay here much longer you won't be going anywhere, except back to the condo where I can have my way with you!"

As he continued the drive, John thought to himself, *Too bad there are people like Dan who can't see beneath Gus' crusty exterior to the beautiful person she is underneath. Yet, Jessie sees it. I could tell by the way they related—even in the short time I saw them together. Go figure!*

Chapter 26: The New Gus Appears: Tuned Up and
Toned Down

Bertha took one look at Gus when she arrived to
pick up Jessie but said no more than a calm hello. Gus'
new situation was all over the school by now. Amanda
hadn't been able to resist telling Doreen about the new
man in Gus' life. And Doreen had told Bertha and
Bertha had lost track of how many people she'd told.

When Jessie and Gus opened the classroom door,
there was a sudden awkward hush. She wondered what
that was all about. The topic for today's class was the
history of dramas about love lost. Brian Littner, the
drama teacher, mentioned that apart from
Shakespeare's *Romeo and Juliet,* there were many
stories about unrequited love.

"Then why did you choose *Romeo and Juliet* for us
to study?" one student asked.

"It's a story of teenage love and you're teenagers.
You should find it interesting."

"But one of our class members is *not* a teenager,"
another student said. There was a sudden hush.

The first student suggested, "Why do we need to
study a love story from so long ago? Why not one that
is happening *now*?"

They're beginning to sound like a tag team! Gus
thought nervously.

And tag! The second student said, "We have a love
story happening right in this *room*. Why don't we write
it up with Ms. Kalline's help and then we can present it

at the general assembly in the spring instead of moldy old *Romeo and Juliet*?"

There was a general chorus of *yeses* from the rest of the class and Gus blushed furiously. Brian Littner looked at her sympathetically but couldn't prevent a little quirk at the corner of his mouth. All eyes were on Gus and suddenly Jessie gave a delightful little laugh.

"You're supposed to be on my side, Jessie!" Gus hissed, but loudly enough to be heard. The whole class, Brian Littner included, roared with laughter. But when the laughter died down, Mr. Littner did his job as a teacher and set about asserting class control. He knew that the best way to deal with this situation was not to pretend that it hadn't happened, but to bring it out in the open so it could then be set aside.

Brian turned to Gus compassionately and said in a humorous tone, "Ms. Kalline, it is apparent you have been outed. Would you care to come up and share just a little of what has been happening in your life recently with the rest of the class so we can then move on to today's lesson?"

Gus, who usually enjoyed the limelight so much, trembled visibly. The old Gus would have attempted to squelch the whole scenario with a haughty remark. But the new Gus remembered that she had friends now, a mystery to solve and a special man back in her life that appeared to care for her very much. She enjoyed the drama class with Jessie and could tell that Jessie enjoyed it, too. But if she made a fool of herself and felt too embarrassed to come back to class she could just opt out and get Jessie's school assistant, Bertha, to replace her.

"May I bring Jessie with me?" she asked. Gus knew that if she could just hold onto Jessie's hand while she talked she would feel more grounded.

Brian nodded and Gus stood up to go to the front. Another student rushed over to wheel Jessie up for her, a thoughtful gesture that made Gus feel a little less threatened. The class became very quiet as she stood there and she clasped Jessie's hand convulsively. And with a sudden thrill, she felt Jessie gripping back as if she understood. Gus immediately felt more centered and quickly rehearsed in her mind what she could say to satisfy the student's curiosity without revealing too much. Obviously she wouldn't be telling them about the bathtub!

"I met John recently quite by accident at a meeting where I was attending to some of my financial affairs. We had been very, very close many years ago". (Gus did not think it necessary to say exactly how many. Her age was not their business!)

"Although we'd been apart a long time, we never forgot each other and the moment we met and looked into each other's eyes, we knew we had made a mistake back then."

Gus dared to look around at her audience then and saw that they were all listening avidly. A few girls even had tears in their eyes. Gus remembered how preoccupying romance was as a subject for teenagers. She also realized at that moment that they weren't laughing at her. They actually looked happy for her! The old Gus would have gushed forth then, over-sharing, thinking of them as her friends. But the new Gus remembered Amanda's frequent warning about her role in Jessie's drama class. Never say too much!

"John and I are planning to marry soon. We can't make up for the lost years but we can at least maximize whatever time we have left together." Gus stopped talking then and one or two students started clapping. Then the rest joined in and then they all stood up. Gus nodded her head at them gratefully, not knowing what else to do. She grabbed Jessie's chair and headed back to her own seat.

Brian took over then. "Thank you so much, Ms. Kalline, for sharing that very touching story. We all wish you and John a very happy future together! He turned back to the class and said, "Well, you have now had your chance to hear about a love story happening in real time. It has many of the elements of the classics: love, love lost, sadness, regret, love regained and new found happiness. It was very generous of Ms. Kalline to share her personal story with us and it should help you to better appreciate what Romeo and Juliet were going through."

"Why don't we just ditch *Romeo and Juliet* and develop her story into a play, instead?" the student who'd spoken earlier persisted.

Brian talked over the murmurings of support he heard for this idea. "First of all, Ms. Kalline would have to agree and I don't think she would." He looked at her and the rest of the class followed his gaze. Gus shook her head vigorously. Jessie's head waved back and forth in solidarity.

"Secondly," Brian went on, "*Romeo and Juliet* is part of the literary canon decreed by the curriculum gods who rule over us to be the most appropriate play to work on with grade 8 drama students."

"What do you mean by 'the literary canon,'" another student asked.

Brian explained, as would any good teacher, recognizing that he had a teachable moment. But he had a second motive. He wanted to get the attention off Gus and devote the remainder of his class to academic discussion to better serve both their needs.

Chapter 27: Hidden Computer Files

When Gus returned home later that afternoon she was anxious to tell Amanda about what had happened in class. However, Amanda and Matthew were poring over computer files together and she certainly wasn't going to discuss it in front of him!

"I've arranged a meeting with the team at Roscoe's house at four," Amanda said. Matthew and I are going to share what we've discovered then."

"Okay," Gus said. "I have a little to report, too. Meanwhile, I'll go to my room and start packing."

"You're leaving?" Amanda asked, looking concerned.

Gus looked at Amanda then, realizing that had been an insensitive way to tell her. "Can Matthew spare you for a few minutes so we can go to my sitting room and talk?"

Amanda looked at Matthew who just nodded his head and went back to transferring the files he'd downloaded on a memory stick onto Amanda's computer so he could print out copies of some of them for the team meeting.

Amanda grabbed a couple of bottles of water from the fridge and her cookie jar and they headed downstairs. Her first comment to Gus was, "I see you got some new clothes. Nice outfit!"

Gus started explaining then, sharing her feelings about John and what their future plans were. When she'd finished, and Amanda had offered the appropriate congratulations, Gus commented, "I was surprised that everyone at school seemed to know." She looked meaningfully at Amanda.

Amanda blushed guiltily. "I'm sorry, Gus. I only told Doreen. I thought she'd be discreet. She was, last time!" Amanda was referring to an earlier adventure they had necessarily shared with the secretary at Jessie's school when they'd all worked together to uncover another murderer.

"Well, obviously, she wasn't discreet this time." Gus told her what had happened in the drama class. They talked for a long while then, about all they'd shared together and their mutual desire to remain good friends.

"I'm going to miss you very much," Amanda said sadly. And she realized that she meant it. Living together in such close quarters, Amanda had come to know Gus well. She could see the value in her better than most people who saw her less frequently.

Suddenly, they both thought to look at the clock and saw that they had only a half hour before the meeting. Amanda went back to check on Matthew's progress and Gus turned to her packing, enough to get her through for the next few days. She shivered thinking she'd be seeing John soon. He'd arranged to pick her up after the meeting.

The meeting began with a summary of what had been discovered on the hidden files in Gary's computer and a discussion about what was still missing.

After Amanda explained how with Sean's help they had been able to crack the pass code to the hidden files, Matthew spoke.

"It's clear that Gary or someone else was trying to erase these files. Even after I got in, I had to do considerable digging to come up with something and then it was only fragments a lot of the time."

"Well, what did you find then?" Gus asked impatiently, her old irritable self temporarily re-emerging. Claire, Tia and Amanda all grinned. Apparently, the happy glow of this new relationship had not completely transformed Gus!

Matthew looked confused, not understanding the in-joke, but moved on. "The files appear to be about financial investments. Like I said, there are the remains of six different files and I'm not sure if they are all talking about the same company or different companies or individuals. I was only able to pull up a few words and phrases of each." Matthew pulled out a few papers and passed them to Amanda to hand around. "This is what I was able to get before the police came for the computer. We told them the password so they may get more."

"It's unlikely they'll share any information with us, though," Claire said. By this time, everyone was looking at the single page they'd received in confusion.

"What Amanda and I thought was if we go through these together," said Matthew, "somebody might come up with something. Okay, here goes: Thr ... Hell's A ... ansf ... f ... ho ... mo c. g. cco ... t ... xt ... udit ... 325,000 ... maica."

After some moments of collective staring, Claire said tentatively, "I think that first phrase is *Hell's Angels*, but what the word in front of it is, I don't know. *Three? Through?*"

"We wondered that, too," Amanda said. "Maybe it'll make more sense if we figure out some of the other phrases."

"Well the last one could be *Jamaica*—and taken together with *Hell's Angels* that might have to do with money laundering or offshore accounts," Tia offered.

"Look at the phrase after *Hell's Angels*," Gus said excitedly. That could be *transfer off shore*!"

"You're right!" Matthew said slowly. "I've been staring at that all day and I didn't see it! Good one, Gus!"

"A fresh pair of eyes always helps," Gus said with surprising modesty. But secretly she was very pleased with herself—and Matthew had gone up considerably in her estimation!"

Meanwhile, Tia had continued to stare determinedly at the fragments. "You see that *udit*? That could be *audit*."

Claire was following on her own paper. "Then the *xt* before it could be the end of *next—next audit*!"

"So this is all about money and maybe hiding money," Matthew speculated.

"Yes, it looks that way. But it really isn't enough to go on. I wonder if Gary had the complete files stored elsewhere—maybe on a memory stick in his office?" Claire mused.

"Maybe John can get in there tomorrow and look," Claire offered.

And with that the meeting broke up.

Chapter 28: Another Break-In

It was the next morning and John planned to go into the office around ten. His time with Gus was too special to feel it necessary to rush out the door any earlier. They woke naturally around 8:30 to the smell of coffee coming from the kitchen. He wrapped his arms around her and then let her go regretfully so that they could prepare for the day and not keep Betty waiting with their breakfast. *Maybe I can arrange for Betty to come in later*, John was thinking. We really are quite capable of getting our own breakfast and I prefer not to have these elaborate breakfasts anyway. I think some privacy in the morning would be good.

They'd just sat down to breakfast when the phone rang. "Hello, Dad. It's Sean. I just phoned to tell you there's no point in coming in this morning. Gary's office was broken into last night and it's a big mess!"

John put the phone on speaker and Sean continued, "The police are here now checking for evidence and Inspector McCoy is up in arms because his Sergeant didn't get the search organized earlier."

In the background Sean heard Gus saying, "It's McCoy's own fault. He didn't believe that the car accident was murder and he dismissed the break-in at Hilda's house as just a random robbery. He as much as told his sergeant just to do a quick check of Gary's office when he got around to it."

Sean was listening to this and snorted in disgust. "Well, he better take it seriously now. Files are all over the floor, Gary's office computer was destroyed and some hard copy files appear to be missing from what we've been able to tell so far. Gary's assistant, Jim Davies, is in there with the police trying to figure out just what."

"Well, so much for us trying to find a lead there," John said resignedly.

"I'm not so sure," Gus interrupted. "Sean, you mentioned that Gary played racquetball quite often. Is it possible that he had a locker at the gym?"

"I don't know," Sean answered, "but I could ask Dave Stout. He's the one who played racquetball with Gary."

"No! Don't do that!" Gus implored. "We don't know who we can trust at this point. If something funny is going on, Gary might not have been the only one at that firm who was involved."

"I could ask the receptionist? Maybe he told her."

"No!" Gus said peremptorily. "We can't be sure of anybody there."

"Well, then, how…wait a minute," Sean mused. "I seem to recall that he left me contact information once when he was going there and his cell was dead and he was expecting an important call from a client. I'll check through my past emails and see if I still have it and get back to you."

"Please do it now and get back to us right away," Gus said. "We need to move fast. Whoever broke into Gary's office may know about his racquetball habit and think about the locker possibility."

'Okay, I'll get started," Sean said, and hung up the phone.

"Even if you get the name of the club, what are you going to do about getting into his locker if he has one—even if you know which locker he has? Besides, it's probably a men's club," John argued.

"Let's go sit in your office," Gus said, aware that Betty was still hustling around, clearing up the breakfast dishes.

Once they were settled in John's home office, Gus picked up the phone and called Amanda. She told her what had happened and asked, "Do you think we could ask Matthew to join that club and then ask around about Gary and find out his locker number and break into it? Do you think he could do that and do you feel you could ask him to do that? You'd have to keep it from his parents."

Amanda demurred for a minute but finally said she'd run it by him. In a few minutes, she phoned back to say that Matthew was excited at the prospect of helping out in this way but needed to know the combination for the lock. "I'm going to ask Hilda," Amanda said. "Maybe she'll know or at least have an idea."

Hilda was surprisingly quick to respond to Amanda's request. "I think you can try that birthday combination again. Gary was born on the 19th of the 9th month in 1981. He always liked playing around with those numbers like I told you when you were looking for the computer password. It didn't work there but it might work for his locker—and I know he had one because he used to take an extra shirt to change into after his workout as well as shampoo and deodorant and a towel and extra underwear so he could have a shower."

When Amanda returned home, Matthew was back from school. He was lounging on the sofa avidly reading book two of the *Lord of the Rings Trilogy*. This was an interest he'd acquired after his involvement in on-line gaming of the Dungeons and Dragons variety with several friends.

Amanda blurted out this information and Matthew quickly put the book down to discuss the situation with her but just then the phone rang.

"Amanda!" Hilda said. "After you left I remembered that Gary lost his combination lock and replaced it with one with a key. I checked his dresser and I found the key and the locker number is right on it, 28!"

"Great!" Amanda replied. "I'll drive over now and pick it up!"

"No, I'll bring it over," Hilda replied. "And you and I and Matthew can discuss what's the best way to do this. I might have some more information that could help."

Amanda agreed and sat back to wait for Hilda. In the meantime she phoned Gus to let her know what was happening. Matthew picked up his book and furtively read a few more pages while he waited for the impromptu meeting to get underway.

"Wow!" was all Gus could say at first. "I hope it works." She felt a twinge of envy not to be in on this adventure but then looked over at John sitting comfortably in his recliner and working his way through a Sudoku puzzle. *No. I wouldn't trade this for my old life,* she thought to herself. Out loud she said, "I guess Hilda's getting a little better if she was willing to come over."

"I think so," Amanda said softly. "I think it helps her to feel like she's doing something to find the murderer."

Chapter 29:   Matthew Demonstrates his Criminal
Tendencies

After Hilda turned over the key, she and Matthew sat
back and listened while Amanda phoned the Century 1
Racquetball Court. "Hello. I'm calling to find out if my
16-year-old grandson who's now living with me can
sign up for a few racquetball lessons at your gym,"
Amanda explained to the receptionist.

"We don't actually give lessons and our clientele
consists primarily of men in their 30's and 40's. But
he's welcome to come here and practice. There's
usually somebody around who wants to play a game.
The club fees are $50.00 a month and the locker rental
is an additional $10.00. Does he have his own racquet?"

"Yes," Amanda said quickly, although she had no
idea if that was the case. She just thought the whole
thing would sound more plausible that way.

"Well, he's welcome to come in and register any
time. It's the 20th of January today but if he wants to
come in and get started he can just pay $15.00 for the
rest of the month."

"Thank you. I'll let him know and we'll set
something up," Amanda said weakly and hung up the
phone. Subterfuge was not her long suit. Gus seemed to
be better at that and if she'd been there, Amanda would
have had her make the call. She missed Gus.

After checking with Matthew that yes, he was
willing to go any time and no, he didn't have a racquet,
Amanda turned to Hilda and asked her if Gary's racquet
was at home. "No," Hilda replied, choking up a bit. "He

always kept it in his car since he never knew when he'd feel like going and generally went straight from work."

Amanda immediately regretted asking and said quickly, "Never mind. I'll call Gus. Maybe John has a racquet. I heard him mention that he played for a while at one point. She called Gus then, who turned immediately to John.

"I have a racquet he can use," John said. "I always thought I might start playing again someday even though I didn't like it all that much. I'll just go and dig it out. And tell Amanda not to worry about the fees. I'll cover them. And if Matthew wants to keep going after he gets whatever information he can, I'll look after that as well. Might be good for him!"

Gus passed this information onto Amanda, awed by his generosity and even more so that he had the kind of money that allowed him to be that generous. This had not been her world. Hilda went home then and later that evening Gus and John dropped the racquet off.

Fortunately, Matthew had had the opportunity to try his hand at racquetball a few times so he wasn't a total novice and Saturday morning, two days later, Amanda and Matthew left the house at 8 o'clock so he could get to the gym early and there would, hopefully, not be too many people there. Amanda then left to do some shopping and asked Matthew to call her cell when he was ready to return home.

The obvious thing would have been for Hilda to go to the gym, herself, explain what had happened and retrieve Gary's possessions. But she wasn't ready to do this yet and Gus kept urging that there was no time to waste. Thus 16-year-old Matthew had been given the key and the mission, despite the fact that somewhere there was a murderer running around loose. Amanda made him promise not to tell his parents.

At the gym, Matthew took his time getting changed, waiting for fewer people to be around. Then he walked nonchalantly to Gary's locker, opened it and scooped out the contents—shorts, a t-shirt and a pair of runners––into the large gym bag he'd brought with him. But when he ran his hands to the back of the shelf to make sure there was nothing he'd overlooked, his fingers felt the distinctive shape of a memory stick.

Matthew palmed the memory stick and placed his hand casually in his shorts' pocket, hoping that none of the two or three men hanging around that section had noticed his action. He placed the gym bag in his own locker some distance away but kept the memory stick with him when he went to the court to play. But when he returned to his locker an hour later, he could see that the lock on his locker had been forced open and his gym bag rummaged through.

Matthew dressed quickly, collected all his and Gary's possessions in his gym bag and left the gym, checking over his shoulder to make sure he wasn't followed. He caught a bus that was just passing and noted that a man who'd been behind him ran to catch the bus but missed it. His heart pounding, Matthew got off in front of a busy department store downtown and quickly walked through it, exiting out the other side. He saw an LRT (light rail transit) entrance across the street, Edmonton's version of a subway, and walked down the stairs there to access it. He purchased a ticket and took the LRT to Southgate Shopping Center, calling Amanda on the way to pick him up.

Once they were safely home, Amanda called Gus to tell her what had happened. Gus had advised Amanda to provide a false address and false last name when she registered Matthew and now Amanda was glad she had. Matthew was unable to provide any descriptions of the men in the gym or to say whether or not the man running to catch the bus had been one of them. They all agreed he should not return to the gym and they should just focus instead on the memory stick he had found.

Chapter 30: Let's Crack Another Code

It turned out that all their struggles with decoding from the computer had been for nothing, because all six files were openly recorded on the memory stick. It was evident that Gary had been working with a number of different individuals or companies to assist them in transferring their assets offshore for tax evasion purposes. Whether or not this was technically legal was unclear. Certainly, the morality of it was in question.

Amanda called Gus and explained what had happened. "Can you come over for the night? And I think I should call Hilda and ask her to come over for a couple of hours, too. She can probably figure out these files better than any of us since accounting is her area."

Later that evening, the four of them sat at Amanda's dining room table methodically reviewing the six files. Five of the files were clearly concerned with offshore transfers. "I recognize Gary's accounting style and some of his turns of phrase," Hilda said sadly. "This is definitely his work. No wonder he was so secretive all the time." She studied the sixth file for a long time. Its rows of figures were a complete mystery to the rest of them.

Finally, Hilda spoke. "I don't think this file is Gary's work. See how the spacing between the columns is different and how the dates are denoted differently? And this file has nothing to do with off shore investing. I think it's the draft for a double ledger for money laundering purposes and *that* is definitely illegal."

"On the other five files, the names of the persons involved are listed but I don't see any names here, only numbers. Do you see anything in the file to indicate where the money would be coming from?" Gus asked Hilda.

"It's from a numbered company but there's no way of telling who the owners are from that."

"I could try to do a search," Amanda said, looking at her computer. "Matthew, do you have any idea how we could find out?"

"I'd have to break into the computer system of the city registry office for small businesses."

"That won't work," Hilda said. "Under our former provincial government, municipal registries were decentralized and privatized. There are at least a dozen different registries in Edmonton."

"There has to be one complete set of records somewhere surely," Gus argued. "What about a provincial registry?"

"Maybe," Hilda replied.

"I'll check," Amanda said, and she started clicking away furiously on her laptop. But in a few minutes she had to admit defeat. "It requires a password," she said. "Apparently, it's not open to the public. That doesn't seem right."

"It's probably to prevent companies from spying on their competitors," Hilda explained.

"Let me try," Matthew begged. "I know a few tricks for cracking passwords!"

"Just don't tell your parents—or brag about it to anybody else, for that matter," Amanda warned.

"Right now I don't know anybody here so you're safe!" Matthew responded, and turned his attention to the computer.

"Hilda, can you think of any clues that might work for the password?" Matthew asked.

Hilda considered the issue for a couple of minutes and then responded, "A big buzzword in the business world this year is *fracking* and a common technique for including numeration that is easily remembered is to put a *0* before and a *0* after the word."

"Hmm," Matthew said. "We'll only get three tries so we better be careful."

"How about *FrackTrack?*" Amanda suggested. "That sounds like some clever thing somebody might think about."

"It's definitely worth a try," Matthew agreed. "I'll put the *0*'s before and after like Hilda suggested." Matthew did this but the site did not open. The four of them sat back in frustration.

"Wait a minute," Gus said. "Who's to say the *0*'s are right? How about the year? *15?*"

"Too obvious!" Amanda said.

"Maybe not," Matthew argued, and he quickly typed in *FrackTrack15*—but it didn't open.

"We have one try left!" Hilda reminded them.

"Maybe using the year was too obvious," Gus conceded, "but if you wanted to use it so it would be easy to remember but make it less obvious, you could split it up—*1* at the beginning and *5* at the end."

"Or vice versa," Matthew added, "or you could just put *15* or *51* at the beginning or *51* at the end."

"My office experience with shared passwords is that we try to make them simple enough for everyone to remember but difficult enough so as not to be obvious to others," Hilda offered. "To me, I think *1* at the beginning and *5* at the end sounds like something bureaucrats might try."

"Okay!" Matthew agreed. "Here goes!" He typed in the new passcode and it opened!

"Wow! We're good!" Amanda crowed.

Chapter 31: A New Mystery Emerges

The Alberta numbered company 104653961-A was categorized as a subsidiary of a larger company, Aspen Construction. Its stated purpose was to build the interior wall units for portable homes and to incorporate the agreed upon amenities: slate fireplaces, kitchen cupboards, and granite kitchen counters, for example. No directors were listed. The Vice-President of Aspen Construction apparently ran the subsidiary company. A private backer was referred to but not named.

"Well, where do we go to from here?" Gus asked in frustration.

"Why don't we look further into Gary's clients, the overseas investors?" Hilda asked. That will at least give us a place to start.

"I can keep working on those files," Matthew offered, "and see what I come up with."

"It was agreed and the meeting broke up. But Gus and Amanda talked long into the night. Gus had so much to tell her and she realized suddenly what it was like to have a real friend who valued her for her strengths and forgave her for her foibles.

The next morning, Matthew went off to school and Gus and Amanda played around with the files on their own, carefully saving them first on a memory stick and using that version to fiddle with so as not to inadvertently damage the original copy. It turned out all five companies were registered at the same city registry, and they found that suspicious. They were able to track down the owners of each account and carefully recorded their names: Jerry Nickerson, Ron Basco, Benni Almaro, Fil Deijers and Mike Miller.

"We need to do background checks on them," Amanda said. Gus looked on silently as Amanda entered each of their names, followed by the word, *Edmonton*, in Google.

"Oh!" Amanda exclaimed suddenly. "Three of them are what's called *full patch* members of the Outriders Hell's Angels Motorcycle Club. But I can't find anything on the other two—Fil Deijers and Mike Miller."

"Could they belong to a different club, maybe one in Red Deer or Grand Prairie or another one in Edmonton?" Gus offered tentatively. "We could visit the Outriders Club and see if we could connect with any of them. Then we could ask them if they knew the other two."

"Uh, I don't think we'd be very welcome," Amanda pointed out. "Maybe we better wait and see what Claire and Tia have to say."

"Tia is going to say, 'Hand it over to McCoy to deal with' and Claire is going to tell us it's too dangerous. What are we? Children? Let's just go—before they have a chance to object!" Gus said impulsively.

"And John? What would John say?" Amanda asked.

"He's not my boss!"

"Yet!" Amanda commented dryly. Then she added, "Gus, I see you looking at my computer. It's not really that hard to learn, especially if you get an Apple. And that way Matthew could help you. I'm sure he'd be okay with that. Also you can take unlimited Apple lessons for a modest price per year and those young people are really sharp—and very patient. Why don't we wait to discuss this other matter with Claire and Tia and focus on getting you a computer while you still have a little time free from John? I'm sure he'd be impressed. And you already have good secretarial skills. You might as well use them."

Gus thought about this for a minute. She suddenly realized that one of the reasons she was still feeling a little uncomfortable around John was that she didn't like being in a one-down position. Having a computer and knowing how to use it would place them on a more level playing field. "Okay," she said abruptly. "Let's go. Where's the Apple store?"

"There's one at Southgate. But I warn you…all Apple stores are zoos with excited young people roaming around, and befuddled older people, that is, anyone over 35, asking for help. When we get there, you snag a computer. They're all chained down to the tables and usually they're being monopolized by the local teens. I'll get hold of a salesclerk and tell him or her that you want to buy a computer today. That will get their attention!"

They did just that and soon the only question was whether Gus should buy a 13-inch or 15-inch MacBook Pro. Gus couldn't be convinced that the 13-inch and 15-inch laptops had identical, full-sized keyboards. Finally, she decided on the 15-inch, feeling that she'd be more comfortable working on the larger surface with the larger screen—and also that it would be more impressive!

Due to a recent cancellation, Gus was able to arrange for her first lesson the very next day and she returned to Amanda's house with her new computer encased in its new computer sleeve. She was hoping to have a serious pre-lesson from Matthew so she wouldn't appear too naïve when she arrived at the Apple Store the next day for her official lesson.

Matthew was happy to help her get familiar with the basics of her new laptop when he returned from school that day but before very long, he needed to retire to his room to do his homework. However, he'd helped Gus to download a Mac tutorial for beginners and she spent several more hours going through the video and practicing. She wrote down a number of questions to put to her Mac tutor the next day during her lesson time and then went to bed happy, content that she wouldn't come into her lesson acting stunned and overwhelmed. Gus had a great fear of looking stupid.

John picked Gus up the next day after her lesson and the following two days passed in a happy blur that does not need to be too fully documented here. Gus spent many hours practicing on her new computer and exploring the glories of the net. She researched everything she could find on Hell's Angels in Edmonton, off-shore tax shelters and money laundering. On Thursday evening, she announced that she needed to spend the weekend with Amanda. John and Gus would be leaving in less than a week for the cruise and she had some loose ends in her life that needed to be dealt with before then. Gus didn't specify what they were.

Friday morning, John regretfully drove her over to Amanda's house but he brightened a bit when she asked him to pick her up in time for Sunday brunch. They agreed to try out a long-time Edmonton favorite: Barb and Ernie's. Gus had been intrigued by Ernie's reputation for flirting with all his female customers and she wondered if he'd flirt with her. Since she'd be dressing at Amanda's house she'd have the freedom to dress as she pleased!

Chapter 32: Time for Action

When Gus arrived Amanda was surprised and didn't look entirely happy to see her. "Oh, Gus! I wasn't expecting you."

"Do I have to be expected? I still live here, don't I? At least until the end of the month when my rent is due?"

"Uh, it's not that. It's just that my cousin invited me to visit her and meet her new grandchild and I'm leaving tomorrow morning for Brandon, Manitoba. I'll be gone all weekend."

"O-o-h," Gus said, accusingly. "I didn't know."

"Well, I didn't know you were planning to visit either," Amanda responded rather tartly. "You haven't spent much time here lately!"

Gus looked around. "Is Matthew here?"

"Yes. He's in his room studying. He's going to drive me to the airport in the morning and pick me up Sunday afternoon. I told him he could have the use of my car while I'm gone if he's careful with it."

"Oh, I see," Gus said. Amanda looked at her suspiciously. "Well, I have a lot of packing and sorting to do this weekend anyway because I'll be moving in with John permanently once we're back from the cruise," Gus explained. "We'll be married then."

Gus turned away then and went to her room. But later on, Amanda knocked on her door and they talked again for a long time. *I'm going to miss her,* Gus thought, after they'd finally said good night to each other. *I can't remember when I've felt so much like I had a real friend. There was Marion, of course, but we didn't really think alike on a lot of things. Basically, she was too nice for me to feel really comfortable around her for very long. I hope that apart from everything else, I can feel this kind of friendship with John. I hope it's not just infatuation as Amanda is suggesting.* But there was also another conversation going on in Gus's head.

By the time Gus woke up the next morning, Amanda was gone and, as she was eating her breakfast, she heard the garage door opening, meaning that Matthew had returned from driving her to the airport. Gus quickly did a mental rehearsal of her strategy.

Gus greeted him with surprising cheerfulness. "Hello," he said, yawning. "We had to be there at 7:30 for a nine o'clock departure. Today was worse than school mornings," he grumped.

"Well, what can I get you? Bacon and eggs? Pancakes?"

Matthew looked at her suspiciously. Gus was not known for either her cooking or her generosity of spirit. "What do you want, Gus—another computer lesson?" As he spoke, Matthew reached for the box of Raisin Bran and got the milk and orange juice out of the fridge.

"No, thanks. I have another Apple lesson scheduled for Tuesday. I think they like the idea down there of teaching an old lady new tricks!" Under normal circumstances, Gus never alluded to her age but there was a lot at stake here and she needed to get on Matthew's good side.

"What, then?" he asked laconically.

"Well, now that you mention it, there is something." Matthew just raised his eyebrows and Gus went on bravely. "You know that we're stuck on this mystery business. The only way we're going to move ahead is through action. I thought of a plan but I need your help to pull it off."

"Listen, Gus. I like risk and adventure as well as anyone, maybe even more than most. But I can't afford to screw up again. Staying with Amanda is like my last chance!"

"Oh, I don't want you to do anything that could possibly place you at risk or get you into trouble. I just need you to drive me over to the Hell's Angels Clubhouse and wait for me. And if I don't come out in an hour or contact you, call Inspector McCoy. I have his number. And if you see me leaving with someone just tail us—at a distance so they don't catch on. That's all!"

"Are you crazy? You can't do that! What would you say to them? If you tell them what you're really after you could place yourself at serious risk!"

"No! I have a plan!"

"Well, it doesn't matter anyway. I have to write a stupid 20-page essay on the contrasting views of the Americans and the British on which of their Generals' battle strategies ultimately led to the Allied victory in World War II. I've got to spend the day researching and writing a draft and even if I work all weekend at it, I doubt that I can get it done in time!"

But Gus was desperate and determined and she began negotiating with him. "Look! When I was checking around on the net I came across this essay site. I'll buy you an essay if you'll do this for me. It's the perfect opportunity with Amanda gone. All she wants to do is get McCoy involved and that has never helped us much in the past!"

"You want me to plagiarize an essay!" A. That's just wrong and B. I'm sure to get caught and then either fail the course or get expelled. In your searching did you happen to come across Turn-It-In? You can't get away with stuff like that anymore."

"Well, no—not exactly," Gus said defensively. "But if we did find an essay on your topic or close to it we could check out the references and then we could pick apart the essay and add bits and pieces and do some rewording. I'm really good with the words. It's one of my strengths. I was a secretary for many years and I used to virtually re-write many of my boss's letters and he came to trust me a lot to do that for him!"

"We-ell," Matthew said. He was really not looking forward to writing this *stupid* essay. "First we find the essay and then if it looks like something we can work with, you tell me your plan. And if your plan isn't too crazy, I'll help you."

"Good!" Gus said, and they got busy searching for the perfect essay. In the process, they accidentally did a lot of legitimate research and at a certain point Matthew realized that this essay could get written with Gus' help whether or not somebody had written on this exact topic—and it was becoming increasingly apparent that no such essay existed since it was an unusual topic. He wondered suddenly if his teacher had chosen this off-beat topic on purpose to prevent plagiarism. Finally, he gave up looking and asked Gus to describe her plan.

"That is just nuts!" he expostulated when she'd finished telling him.

"No! I'm pretty sure it can work. I'm a good actor. That's another one of my strengths. And I can't see any other way to move forward."

Matthew was in a dilemma. Now that he had time to think it through, he realized that he really wanted and needed help with that essay. And Gus' plan did have its points—and besides, it would be very exciting. Finally, he agreed and Gus went off happily to prepare herself for her debut at the Hell's Angels Clubhouse. But she carried her computer with her, still connected to the Wi-Fi from Amanda's server, and before she got down to selecting her clothes for this adventure, Gus did some further research on bikes.

Chapter 33: Gus makes Inquiries

When Gus came out of her bedroom dressed and ready to go meet the gang at the motorcycle club, Matthew was appalled. "You can't go like that!" he blurted. "You look ridiculous!"

Gus was crestfallen. She'd put a lot of effort into constructing her outfit and thought that she looked very hip, like a biker chick—and she said as much.

"But you're not a biker chick!" he replied, with teenage bluntness. "If anything, you're a biker granny——but I don't think there are any of those." He looked again at her get-up: aged, form-fitting blue jeans, black, leopard-print short cowgirl boots with pointed toes, and a fitted long-sleeved, red plaid shirt with silver snaps up the front. It was tucked into her jeans and cinched with a western style belt with a big silver buckle. Gus looked very trim and upright in it, thanks to the rigors of her corset. But her stiff movements and wrinkled face were in stark contrast to the effect she was trying to create.

"Look," Matthew said, not unkindly. "My understanding of telling lies or putting on an act successfully is that you have to say or reveal as much that is actually true as possible. Trying to pretend that you have the mojo of a 20-year-old doesn't fit that script. Why don't you try for the sympathy approach? The worried grandmother?"

Gus returned to her room. A long time later, she re-emerged, looking very different from her previous apparition. She still looked very svelte. Gus had not parted with the corset for a couple of reasons. However, this was not the chic appearance she'd presented to Sean and then John at their first meeting. This time, she looked her age, but a very dignified, well-kept age. Gus was wearing a sedate grey pantsuit neatly belted at the waist with a shimmery, long-sleeved, soft grey blouse tucked in. On her feet were black leather pumps with a 2-inch block heel. Matthew nodded in approval and they were off. He parked half a block from the clubhouse and Gus walked slowly towards the door. She knocked and waited.

"Who are you?" was the greeting she received from the young man of medium height with long, dark, greasy hair who opened the door.

"Excuse me," Gus said nervously, clutching her small, black handbag firmly under her arm. "I'm looking for my grandson. His mother is critically ill and I'm sure he'd want to see her."

"What's his name?"

"His name is Terence Ferrell but he might be using an alias. He never liked his name very much. When he was at school the other guys used to call him Terry-Fairy. Maybe that's why he grew up to be so tough—to prove something," she babbled.

The man just stared at her and then began to close the door. "Never heard of him," he muttered.

"Wait!" Gus begged. "I know he would've come here! There were three different guys he always talked about and he told me they all belonged to this club. He was riding a Harley-Davidson 2013 Sportster. Does that help?"

"Humph! Not much of a bike. What made him think he could play in the big leagues?"

"He's only 20. That was all he could afford. But he said he was going to get himself some big money soon and buy a better bike. I don't know how he could get money like that legally, though. You can see why we're worried!"

With a sneer on his face, the young man said, "There's a church down the street. Maybe you better go there. We're not into sad stories here!"

"I want to talk to those guys he mentioned," Gus said firmly. "One of them must have seen him."

"Who?"

"Jerry Nickerson, Ron Basco and Benny Almaro."

"Jerry!" he yelled over his shoulder—but there was no answer. "Just a sec," he muttered and left the room. Gus quickly grabbed her cell phone and called Matthew on speed dial. He had programmed it into her phone earlier.

"I'm fine. Another hour. Meeting Jerry," she said and she shut the phone and tucked it away just in time as she saw the first young man approaching with another.

"Yeah. I'm Jerry. What da ya want?" Gus told him her story and looked at him pleadingly.

"Nope, nobody like that has come around here."

"But somebody must know! What about Ron Basco? Is he here?"

"Listen, lady. This is not a halfway house or a shelter. We don't take in strays!" Jerry retorted, and began to close the door.

"I guess I'll have to go to the police, then, and get them to come out here. I know he must have come here!"

"Fine, I'll get Ron. But he's going to tell you the same thing." As he turned to leave, Gus grabbed her cell phone and took a quick picture. It was from the back but at least it was something.

In a couple of minutes, a short, stocky man of about 35 came out of the other room and scowled at her. "What do you want with me, lady?"

"I want to know if my grandson, Terence Ferrell, has contacted you?"

"Never heard of him. And I think it's time you left."

"Okay, but I'm going straight to the police station. Terry found your names and that third man's name on his uncle's computer and I know he was looking for you."

"Who was the third guy?" Ron asked.

"Benny Almaro." Ron looked reflexively at the man who'd first opened the door for Gus.

"That's right," he said. "I'm Benny—and none of us have heard of your grandson, so what exactly are you trying to pull here?"

"Terry got his uncle's computer when he died and you were all mentioned there. He knew you were into something big and wanted to be part of it."

"What was his uncle's name?" Jerry said evenly.

"Gary Boaz."

"I think you better come with us," Ron said, and grabbed her roughly by the arm.

Chapter 34: Matthew Gets Worried

It was an hour and a half since Gus' last call and Matthew was wondering what to do. They'd agreed he would call Inspector McCoy, but he called Claire instead. Matthew didn't like the idea of talking to the police.

"Oh, no! I should've known she wouldn't wait," Claire responded. "I've just been so busy at the house trying to get things running properly again. Roscoe went to serve at the restaurant with a big gravy stain on his suit lapel the other day and Daisuke sent him home and re-assigned one of the waiters to cover the front door for the evening. And Bill was trying to juggle the knives at work and one of them fell and cut his hand. It's not serious but it could have been. And Mavis had one of her regular seizures and the new staff person panicked and gave her emergency Ativan. Then she couldn't even wake up enough the next morning to have her regular meds on time and she had a horrible day as a result!"

Claire was babbling and she knew it but she was at the same time trying to think what to do. There was no point in going to the clubhouse alone and demanding the return of her aunt but she hated to call in Inspector McCoy and listen again to his usual scolding speech about interfering. She hung up the phone after promising Matthew she'd take care of it and to stay out of it. "Just go home!" she instructed. "We don't want you involved in any part of this. Amanda would hit the roof!" She hung up her cell phone but just then it rang again.

"Claire, Claire?" came a weak voice over the phone she recognized as belonging to her Aunt Gus.

"Where are you? Tell me quick! Matthew called."

"I don't know. They took me to some warehouse, I think. It seems empty and its cold."

"But where? Did you see anything, any familiar signs or landmarks or street numbers?"

"They put a scarf over my eyes and tied my hands but I managed to wiggle it up so I could see a little." The last time they stopped the car, it was at an LRT crossing. I heard the train and I was able to see the bottom tiers of the Commonwealth Stadium. We only went a couple of blocks after that. Oh! I hear them coming back!" Gus closed her emergency back-up phone and slipped it back inside her corset but she didn't have time to do it up. She just hoped the bulge wouldn't show. She leaned over in a show of dejection and covered her waist with her hands.

Claire disconnected the phone from her end and then called Inspector McCoy. She had no choice. Her aunt's life might be at risk!

"I can't believe you people!" he ranted. "When are you ever going to learn to mind your own business!"

"Save the lecture for later and set up a search for my aunt, please! She's within roughly two blocks of the stadium, likely in an empty warehouse. They were driving from the Outriders clubhouse so they were probably going east."

"I'll see what I can do," he responded, and hung up the phone.

Claire called Tia but she'd been having some false labor pains that morning and was on bed rest just in case. Jimmy was home with her so there was no question of Tia accompanying Claire to search for Aunt

Gus. Claire called in a replacement staff to cover for her and as soon as Jane arrived, she grabbed her purse, left the house and climbed in her car. She was just pulling out of the driveway when the passenger door opened and Matthew jumped in. "I'm going with you!" he said defiantly.

Claire looked at him and thought about resisting but then she realized she just couldn't do this on her own. "Then you better drive," she said. "I don't think I'm up to it," and she exited the car so he could slide over.

Tia phoned her a few minutes later. "I'm on Google Maps. There's an empty warehouse on 80th Street and 113th Avenue and another warehouse at 84th Street just south of 118th Avenue. Where are you?"

"We're on the Whitemud Freeway about to turn up 75th Street. We should reach 111th Avenue in ten minutes if they're finished with the construction on the bridge across the river. Matthew's with me. He insisted on coming."

"Okay, keep in touch." And Tia ended the call. Then she called McCoy to report what was happening and the two addresses she'd given to Claire. She heard him growl and then she heard the car siren come on. *That will get him to move faster!* she thought to herself. Then she looked at her stomach in exasperation. I should be there with Claire. When she gets worried like this, she's likely to do something foolish.

Chapter 35: Showdown!

Claire and Matthew had crossed 101st Avenue where 75th Street turns into Wayne Gretzky Drive and were approaching the off-ramp leading to 112th Avenue. Claire directed Matthew where to go and within minutes they'd pulled up in front of the empty warehouse on 80th Street and 113th Avenue. Claire jumped out of the car and Matthew did too. "No! You stay here!" Claire commanded.

"No way!"

"You should stay so you can call for backup if I don't return—" she started, but he cut her off.

"I'm going!" he cried, as Claire ignored him and headed quickly towards the front door. Matthew stopped long enough to grab the tire iron out of the trunk and then followed her.

The door was locked and they circled the building looking through all the windows but saw nothing.

"It's shut down!" a passerby yelled. "It's been closed for three years."

They ignored him and circled the building again, scrutinizing the basement windows this time, but could see and hear nothing.

"Maybe we better try the other warehouse," Matthew suggested. They headed back to the car and this time Claire drove. Matthew saw a police car pulling up to the abandoned warehouse just as they got back to 112th Avenue, and he told Claire to make the turn onto the Avenue quickly. The passerby must have seen the tire iron and reported them.

They only had a few blocks to go to reach the other warehouse and Matthew called Tia to let her know where they'd been and where they were heading. Tia was grateful that he was with Claire because this was just the kind of caution that would never have occurred to her under the pressing circumstances.

The other warehouse had a more ominous look to it and somehow it didn't seem so empty. They approached it warily from the back and began discreetly peeping in both upper and lower windows as they rounded it. Suddenly, they heard a thud and a woman's scream. A small cell phone came sailing out the window just above them and by a fluke Matthew caught it. They huddled near the wall out of the sight line of any window and examined the phone. "It's not hers," Claire said in relief.

Matthew studied the phone some more and then pointed out a small label that had been attached. It read *Sheridan Investments*. This must be John's phone!"

Claire gasped. "That means..." and she began running towards the door again. She pounded on it imperiously. Matthew started to run after her but then he hung back. If they got Claire, he needed to be able to tell the police where she was. With fumbling fingers he dialed Tia's number and reported what had happened.

"Get off the phone so I can call McCoy," she said tersely, and then hung up.

Don't tell them I'm out here, Claire! We need every advantage we can get! Matthew half thought and half prayed. A long five minutes passed before an unmarked car pulled up beside him. "Matthew turned to the self-important looking slightly built man with the dapper moustache. He assumed this was Inspector McCoy. He definitely had the tough, mean look of a policeman. "Claire is in there—and we think Gus is too! Her phone was thrown out the window up there," he said, pointing.

"Stay here!" McCoy growled. "That's an order!" He turned to Sergeant Crombie who was still in the car and said, "Call for backup and then follow me in!"

"Shouldn't we wait, sir?"

"Wait if you like," McCoy snarled, and then headed for the door. McCoy was a lot of things, but a coward wasn't one of them. He knew he wasn't following correct procedure to go in alone but he also knew that every minute counted.

When he reached the front door, he found it locked and it wasn't the kind of lock that could be picked. He started circling around the warehouse and eventually found a partially open window, conveniently located just over from a dumpster. He climbed up, balancing on the edge of the dumpster, and got as close to the window as he could. Standing on his toes and leaning as far over as was possible, he managed to get both hands on the windowsill and then swing his legs over.

McCoy was able to hoist himself up, thanks to the years of chin-ups he'd done in the gym, and he glanced inside. Nobody was there and he clambered over the sill and fell face forward into the room. He hadn't made much noise but still might have been heard—and it had been quite an effort. He saw a storage closet in the corner and quickly retreated to it to give himself time to recover and to conceal himself in case someone had heard him and came to investigate.

A couple of minutes later, he emerged from the closet, breathing normally and none the worse for wear except for a nasty scrape on one leg. He tiptoed quietly over to a closed door and listened intently. Nothing! McCoy opened it and crept down a hallway, senses alert. He thought he heard a faint rumble above and climbed the stairs, keeping close to the edge to avoid creaks. Through the second door down on that floor he definitely hear voices, threatening voices and an occasional smack. McCoy was brave but not stupid. He stepped back into the stairwell and called Sergeant Crombie on his phone. "How far out are they?"

"Two or three minutes max."

"The men are on the second floor, east end of building, second door down. I thing they're roughing up the women."

This upset Sergeant Crombie who had a real soft spot for Claire. "I'll call them with locator info and join you asap."

"Front door locked. I'll open it now."

Crombie made the call, ordered Matthew to remain in the car and repeat McCoy's directions to the back-up unit when it arrived and headed for the door. But by the time McCoy got the door open, the back-up police were already there, six altogether in two separate cars. Four of them stationed themselves strategically at the exits and the other two accompanied McCoy and Crombie to the upstairs room where they could clearly hear the harsh voices and the whacks. Gun drawn, McCoy shoved the door open and dived in with the others following. It was over very quickly. The three men, later identified as Jerry, Ron and Benny, were subdued and cuffed. Gus and Claire had both been tied up and their faces were red from repeated slaps.

Gus appeared to have passed out and an ambulance was called. When the two medics arrived with the stretcher, she opened her eyes and hissed at them "Wrap a sheet around me before you load me on the stretcher. I think I wet myself." Then she promptly passed out for real.

Gus and Claire were both taken in the ambulance to the hospital to be checked out. Later, Sergeant Crombie interviewed them. Matthew was allowed to return home and he remained on the phone with Tia all the way so she could guide him back. He was in a very shaken state and he was driving through a strange city.

Chapter 36: Consequences

Tia didn't hear anything back from Inspector McCoy
but that didn't surprise her. He was always happy to
receive information but never to give it. She and
Matthew were huddled in Tia's living room discussing
what to do next when the phone rang. It was Claire.

"Tia—I'm okay. Did Matthew make it back okay
with the car?"

Tia put the phone on speaker and replied, "He's here
now, Claire. How are you? And how's Gus?"

"They're keeping her in overnight for observation
but nothing is broken—and I'm fine except for a sore
face. I'm just waiting to see when I'll be allowed to
leave. I'll take a taxi straight there so I can pick up the
car. Dan doesn't need to know about this."

Jimmy had heard the phone and was standing in the
doorway. He walked over and leaned into it now. "I
already called Dan, Claire. He's on his way to the
hospital now."

"Oh," Claire gulped. "Okay." She hung up the phone
and headed for the nearest bathroom to see what she
could do about covering up the red marks on her face.

Jimmy replaced the phone in its cradle and turned to
Tia. "I'm just glad I took the day off because of your
false contractions. Otherwise, you'd probably be in the
hospital too right now!" he growled. Tia just glared at
him and said nothing. Her mind was on what to say to
Amanda—and then there was John. She'd forgotten all
about John!

Claire did not arrive home from the hospital until 8:30 that evening. Their evening assistant, Karen, had agreed to stay with Jessie longer and put her to bed so Dan could pick Claire up.

After Karen left and Jessie was sleeping soundly, Claire told him the whole story. Dan was angry and upset but he didn't know who to be most angry with. He had to admit that it hadn't been Claire's wild scheme that had brought her into danger this time. She'd just been trying to protect her aunt and he couldn't blame her for not trusting McCoy to do the job in time. It was Aunt Gus again! He gritted his teeth thinking of all the trouble she'd caused through the last few years. And now she apparently had an ally—some silly, sixteen year old boy!

Meanwhile, Tia was feeling that she had no choice but to inform John. The plan had been for him to pick Gus up at Amanda's house the next morning, Sunday, at 11 o'clock. If Tia didn't call him now, he'd know that she'd deliberately kept the situation from him and that would make it even worse. She waited until visiting hours at the hospital were over at eight because she was pretty sure that Gus wouldn't want to see him in her present condition. Predictably he was very angry and upset.

Great! Tia thought to herself sourly. Now we have three men trying to control our lives! Let's just hope Amanda doesn't decide to get hooked up or we won't have any leeway left at all to pursue our little adventures.

The next morning, John was at the hospital at nine, demanding impatiently to know when Gustava Kalline would be discharged. But the doctor did not get around to seeing her and signing her discharge papers until 10:30. John then transported her directly back to his condo, refusing to listen to any discussion about returning to Amanda's place to pick up fresh clothing. "There's enough at the Condo," he told her tersely. You can bathe and change while I order in some lunch. We are obviously not going out with you in *that* condition," he said, referring to her bruised and swollen face. "Just put all your clothes in the bathroom hamper and Betty will take care of them."

Finally, they were seated quietly in the large living room of John's luxurious condo. Gus had completed her ablutions and was tucked into a comfortable recliner with a blanket over her knees. She still looked weak and tired. John regarded her with concern but couldn't stop the ranting he was doing. All sorts of strong feelings were roiling around inside him: anger and fear and a sense of betrayal. "How could you do such a stupid thing?" he asked for the umpteenth time. "Did you think those people were just playing games in their clubhouse—like boy scouts? Don't you read the papers?"

Finally, Gus had herself together enough to answer him. "We were stuck. There was no other way forward. And I needed Matthew's help because I don't drive. I did keep him out of it!" she said in her own defense.

John just shook his head, not yet ready to forgive her—but just then the doorbell rang. "I hope you don't mind, John," Claire said. "We just had to see how Aunt Gus was. And Dan, Tia, Jimmy and Matthew trailed in behind her."

"You should be home working on your essay, Matthew," Gus admonished him, her voice still raspy from all the screaming and shouting she'd done the day before.

"It's no use," he said. "I'm just going to call in sick tomorrow and work on it then."

"You send me a draft and I'll fix it up. I'm so sorry. I didn't mean for it to work out like this!" Gus said.

Dan, Jimmy and John collectively rolled their eyes and shared a bonding moment. Claire and Tia snickered when they saw it and Matthew looked confused. Gus snorted angrily and slapped her hand on the table. "Could we all just stop for a minute and consider what we did accomplish, rash as you might think our actions were?"

Claire turned to Gus apologetically. "You're right, Aunt Gus. We really were at a dead end and I don't know how we could've moved forward if you hadn't done what you did. And it was a pretty clever plan actually!"

Gus grinned at finally receiving something other than criticism for her actions. "Now we can get McCoy to grill them about the other two names we uncovered. Kidnapping and assault are pretty serious charges. They're going to want to cooperate!"

"But," Tia said, "we're no closer to finding Gary's and Marion's murderer. Nothing they've said or done points in that direction."

"Coincidences do occur," John offered. "They're obviously into something crooked and Gary was not concerning himself with the source of their income and just abetting them in avoiding income tax. I don't see how that would give them a reason to murder him?"

"They kept asking us who all had seen Gary's records and how we knew him and what we were planning to do with the information but nothing else," Claire volunteered.

"They wanted the original files and they said they didn't know anything about the office break-in," Gus added.

"Well, then. It really does seem like we're back at square one."

"But at least we have three less suspects to worry about, thanks to Matthew and Aunt Gus," Claire pointed out.

"Well, there's one thing I know," John stated firmly. "Gus has made her contribution. We're leaving in a few days and until then I plan to keep her very close to me and safe—so the rest of you are on your own now!"

Jimmy smirked. "Good luck with that, John. You don't know these women. Dan laughed and nodded his head in agreement.

Gus turned to Matthew. "I feel really bad about your paper and I still intend to help you with it. I'm going to begin researching it as soon as I can today and we'll stay in touch by email and by phone. Also, I may have some computer questions for you. Once we get your paper out of the way, I plan to keep working on Gary's files." Gus turned to John then and said rather snippily, "You can't object to me sitting her and working on the computer to find some answers, I trust?"

"No," he said stiffly. "I can handle that—but anywhere you go, I go—until we leave." Gus just rolled her eyes but inside herself she felt two conflicting feelings. It was painful to give up some of her independence but at the same time so wonderful to have a man in her life who cared about her and her wellbeing.

The others in the group looked at each other but then Matthew jumped up. "I have to leave to pick Amanda up at the Airport. I'm already late! I'm going to have to tell her what happened and she's not going to be happy about my role in it."

"I'll talk to her," Gus said, her voice still weak and raspy. "It was not your fault. I pretty much conned you into it and I'll tell her so." John looked at her appreciatively.

Chapter 37: The Ups and Downs of Research

After everybody else left, John and Gus spent some time discussing the case and had to agree that they were not that much closer to discovering the murderer than they'd been before this latest incident.

"But somebody went through Matthew's locker at the gym—and he was pretty sure somebody tried to follow him!" Gus said. "We need to follow up on that somehow."

John just looked at her. "Well, I can tell you who's not going to be following up on that! Anyway, I think the first step to following up on that idea is to get McCoy to include it in his interrogations."

"He's not known for taking our suggestions," Gus said sourly. "But about now Matthew is going to be telling Amanda what happened. He will have to. Once she gets over being angry with him and me, *particularly* me, I'll talk to her about calling Inspector McCoy. She's the only one who seems to be able to get anywhere with him these days!"

"So how do you plan to get on her good side again?" John asked.

"By helping Matthew with his essay. I was planning to do it anyway because I feel really badly about messing him up this weekend. And also, he was in a talkative mood on the way to the clubhouse yesterday morning. His problem is that he's too smart for his own good and has been basically bored in school. He never learned how to study properly because he never had to. He managed to get respectable marks with little or no effort. The only thing he ever put any effort into was learning the ins and outs of computers because that's what he found intellectually challenging. And all that got him was a lot of grief!"

"Well, he wouldn't be the first teenager who defied his parents and decided to go a different way."

"But that's just it. He loves his parents and wants to please them. He's really feeling badly about what happened in Brandon and if he messes up this essay and puts his future here in jeopardy, he'll be very, very unhappy about that."

"Well, you can't exactly write his essay for him!"

"No...but I can do some research for him and teach him how to do research." Gus added in a low voice, "But first I'm going to have to learn how myself on this computer."

John heard and said, "I can help you with that," and Gus looked at him gratefully, struck once again by how absolutely wonderful it was to have someone of your own always at your side for support.

She placed her computer on the long side of the kitchen table and turned it on. They sat down side by side and she looked at it helplessly, not knowing where to begin. "We'll start with Wikipedia," John said, "and then when we find some suitable references, we'll look up the articles on Google Scholar. From there we can get the complete references and then access the articles through the data bases at the university."

"But how do we get into them? Don't you have to be a student or a professor?"

"I'm an alumnus of the University of Alberta and a long time donor. I requested and received full library access some years back. I don't often have occasion to use it because we have our own financial data bases at the office but this would be a good time to see exactly what they have to offer."

John showed Gus how to open up Wikipedia and Google Scholar and then asked her what the essay topic was. Gus furrowed her brow for a moment but then it came to her. "I remember because I thought it was kind of odd for a high school essay. The teacher wants them to research the differences between the American and British contributions that led to the allied victory in World War II in 1945. They would need to look at their respective roles in the various war theatres and the relative efficiencies of their army and air force commanders."

John laughed. "Yeah, I've heard a few Brits pontificating on that subject. The war began in September of 1939 after Germany's attack on Poland. But the U.S. didn't enter the war until December 7th, 1941, after the Japanese bombed Pearl Harbor and destroyed the bulk of the American naval vessels. The way I heard it, once they joined, the allied forces more or less took over, with little regard for the wisdom and experience of the war-seasoned British generals."

"Well, what about Canada? We were there, too!"

"Like Australia, we were more or less viewed by the British as a junior partner. They still had a strong colonial attitude at that time. Remember, the Canadian constitution was not fully repatriated until the passing of the Canada Act by the British Parliament in 1982."

"Well, what about the Soviets, then? I heard that they sustained the heaviest military losses of any of the allies, somewhere between 10 and 13 million soldiers. And there were many civilian deaths as well. My boss was from Belarus, part of the Soviet Union at that time. He told me that Belarus lost 25% of its population in World War II!"

"World War II resulted in the greatest loss of life of any event in human history," John said soberly. "Three percent of the human population at that time." He quickly pulled up a war records site on the internet and scanned it. "Look at that! There were 15 million military casualties and an additional 45 million civilian deaths. And that may be an underestimate. Some historians say there were 50 million civilian deaths in China alone from the Japanese invasion there and nobody here even talks about that in conjunction with the war!"

"So that's why there's such hatred by many Chinese for the Japanese!" Gus replied, and she told John about Roscoe's experiences when he worked at The Piccadilly Fish and Chips Shoppe.

"Well, in any case, from what I've seen so far, there's plenty of material readily accessible on the net for Matthew to use for his essay."

"Yes," Gus said, musing. "And I'm going to help him to frame it within this larger picture. Whatever ego clashing was going on between generals, the fact is that the allies were losing the war at the time America finally joined. It was the Americans' superior resources that ultimately turned the tide. That doesn't change the fact that General Montgomery and others like him were very clever, even brilliant, strategists, but they could only work with what they had."

Gus paused for a moment and then went on. "I'm hoping that in the end Matthew will not only get a good mark on this essay but begin to appreciate what the larger world is about. Then maybe he'll become more interested in advancing his education and I intend to help him do that!" John looked at her admiringly.

Chapter 38: First the Body; Then the Mind

Once John had shown Gus the basics of internet searches, she worked away on her own methodically. She collected references, identified themes and organized a viable structure to effectively address Matthew's essay topic. Then she developed a series of questions. At one point, John did question her rather impatiently. "Do you think it's appropriate to be doing all this work for him?"

"Oh, don't worry," she said. "In the end, he's going to need to incorporate his own thoughts and his own words." John listened in on several phone calls Gus had with Matthew and was surprised at her natural teaching ability. She provided certain information but then led him along to explore and develop ideas on his own. She had him email her drafts of various parts of his essay and critiqued them. In the end, Matthew put his own slant on it and produced a respectable piece of work.

"How did you get that much out of him?" John asked admiringly.

"I've had lots of practice," she replied. "For the last 20 years of my career, I worked for the same boss. He was an effective businessman but a terrible communicator. He actually had a learning disability and couldn't put together a coherent letter to save his soul. I ghost wrote virtually all of his correspondence and it wasn't simply a matter of grammatical correctness either. I actually had to organize his thoughts for him on many occasions. And I had to do it very carefully so that he wouldn't feel threatened or like I was being too pushy."

"It's just unfortunate that you never had the opportunity to go further in university," he muttered.

"I think that's why I've enjoyed working on these murders so much," Gus responded. I like the intellectual challenge of it. And now that I've finally overcome my fear of technology, I'll be able to do a lot of things I couldn't do before. Speaking of which, now that Matthew has his paper under control, I think it's time to do some more research on this murder case before we leave on the cruise."

"I thought you would want to spend these last couple of days shopping. Don't you want to buy some new clothes to take along?"

"Not as much as I want to crack one more of these file names we uncovered," Gus responded, and she was herself surprised by her answer. In the past she'd have been totally preoccupied with outfitting herself appropriately but the challenge of working on this murder puzzle had become much more intriguing to her than the idea of shopping.

"Of the original five files we uncovered from Gary's computer, we haven't yet been able to find information on two of them—Fil Deijers and Mike Miller. You seem pretty skilled in Internet searches. Where would you look?"

"You thought they might also be involved with the Hell's Angels but they aren't in the Edmonton branch. Could they be in some other branch?"

"There are dozens of branches across Canada. It would be very time consuming to search them all. I just keep thinking that if they were using Gary to do their laundering, they must be based here in Edmonton."

"What about other cities in Northern Alberta that might have Hell's Angels' clubs or other motorcycle clubs? They're not the only outfit, you know. Anyway, I'd think that people operating on the wrong side of the law couldn't go to just any accountant to do their work. Some of them might have heard about Gary and been willing to come here to Edmonton to work with him."

"I guess it's a possibility. I'll keep looking." All Monday evening and Tuesday, Gus clicked away methodically, searching for any mention of the two unidentified members and finally her efforts were rewarded. John had showed her how to broaden her Internet search and she discovered a group in Red Deer with many links to the Hell's Angels in Edmonton, but operating under a different name, the Rebel Kings. There she finally ran to earth both of the missing members.

"But how do we get in touch with them?" Gus asked John. "We have no time to go down there."

John smiled and grabbed her computer. He quickly pulled up the Red Deer phone book on the Internet and checked it for the two names. There were 12 Millers listed but only two Deijers. He phoned the first Deijers number and when an older woman answered he said, "Hello. May I speak to Fil."

"We haven't seen him for two or three weeks now. Who's calling please?"

"Oh, just tell him John called when you talk to him. He knows how to get hold of me." John called the other Deijers number then but there was no answer. He turned to Gus. "According to the woman I talked to, this Fil Deijers person hasn't been seen around since the time of the accident so it's possible that he's the dead person in the Van. You better call your friends and tell them what we know and ask them to take it from here!"

Gus sent a group email to Amanda, Tia and Claire outlining what they'd found out and suggesting that someone, Amanda perhaps, phone McCoy and find out if the coroner was able to collect a DNA sample from the burnt body in the Van. If so, he could contact the Deijers family in Red Deer and see about getting DNA from a parent or sibling to look for a match.

Claire phoned a short time later and Gus related the whole story to her. Then Amanda phoned and then Tia phoned. Gus could see that John was getting exasperated with all the phone calls and recognized that this was one more area of freedom she wouldn't have if she carried through with her promise and married him. When John finally went off to bed in disgust, she quickly phoned Claire back and did a bit of venting about her fear of losing her freedom.

"Marriage is definitely a trade-off but it's worth it in the end," was Claire's response. "The trouble with this whole thing with you is that it's happened so quickly. We should have been able to arrange a stagette for you but now there's no time."

"A what?"

Claire explained and then said, "We'll just have to do it backwards and arrange it after you get back. Although really we should be setting up a wedding reception for the two of you."

"No. John doesn't want that and neither do I. If we last a year I think we're going to have a big first anniversary bash! I think it's going to take me that long to get this all figured out. It still doesn't seem quite real to me!"

"It has definitely been a whirlwind romance!" Claire commented, stating the obvious, and doing so in her usual clichéd format.

They said their good nights and then Gus went up to bed where John was still awake and waiting for her.

Chapter 39: The Rebel Kings Connection

When Amanda called Inspector McCoy and shared the information Gus had managed to uncover about Fil Deijers, he was very interested. She was relieved to hear that the coroner had indeed taken a DNA sample before the remains of the man in the Van had been cremated. McCoy immediately contacted the RCMP in Red Deer and asked them to follow up with the family since it was something that needed to be done face to face. Three days later, Amanda received a call back from him.

"I can't tell you any details about the family but the mother and younger brother did provide DNA samples. We just got the results back this morning and our RCMP contact in Red Deer has informed the family that the DNA was a match. Fil Deijers was definitely the driver of the vehicle that killed Gary Boaz and Marion McKay. I have already called Ms. Boaz to tell her the news."

Amanda thanked him for sharing the information and hung up the phone. She wondered how the family had responded, how they were feeling, and if they had any idea why Fil Deijers had done such a thing. She phoned Claire and Tia and they arranged to meet at Roscoe's home right away to decide where they should go from here.

"Why would he do it?" Amanda asked, once they were settled in the living room with coffee and some of her healthy cookies that she'd brought along. Roscoe was in his room working on yet another set of addition exercises.

"Do you ever feel like you're doing Roscoe a disservice by loading him up with all this homework all the time when he could be out in the world experiencing different things, Claire?" Tia asked.

"Yes, but then I think about how well he's doing in his day cashier work at the restaurant and how proud he is when he has an error free day. He's come a long way and I think he can get better still with more practice. We all have to do drudgery at times to achieve our ends and I think Roscoe has to do the same."

"I think you're right," Amanda commented. "There's no satisfaction like the satisfaction of a job well done. Entertainments are fleeting pleasures but a solid sense of accomplishment lasts."

"I'm glad you agree—and now let's discuss this situation because I'm sure Roscoe will be through with those exercises in half an hour. He's getting faster all the time!"

"This Fil guy must have done it for money. Somebody must have hired him and offered him a lot of money to kill Gary and Marion. Why else would he take a crazy chance like that? He was 20 years old and we know he wanted to buy a big bike and become a gang member. That must have been his motivation!" Tia proclaimed.

"Okay, I agree—but who hired him? How are we going to find that out?" Claire asked.

"The only leads we have are those six files. I think it has to be one of those six!" Amanda stated.

"I thought we'd agreed to eliminate three of them," Tia reminded her.

"But we don't really know if we can eliminate them for sure," Claire pointed out, "and McCoy isn't going to share what he got out of interrogating them."

"I'm going to call Sergeant Crombie and ask him. I think he'll tell me something at least," Tia said. "Surely the Red Deer RCMP contact officer has been asking the family what they know. Maybe he'll tell me that if nothing else."

"Its worth a try," Claire replied slowly, "but I still think we need to do more. Ask him if they're planning to talk to any of the members of the motorcycle club down there because if they aren't going to do that, then I think we'll have to."

"After what happened to you and Gus?" Amanda asked incredulously.

"Where else can we go from here?" Claire responded, and the other two had to agree with her.

Then next morning, Tia called Sergeant Crombie and was fortunately able to connect with him when he wasn't busy and when McCoy was out of the office on other business. They had a 15-minute long talk in which the Sergeant disclosed a lot of information.

First, none of the three club members admitted to knowing anybody else who'd used Gary Boaz as an accountant. When asked how they'd heard of him in the first place, Jerry stated vaguely that he'd heard his name floating around somewhere but he couldn't remember where. He admitted that he was the one who'd told the other two in their little threesome about Gary. When asked if he'd passed this information on to anybody else, he said no, even though he was asked the question several times in various interviews. There was no way to know if he was telling the truth or not.

"Did you ask them if Gary had ever mentioned other clients to any of them, like the two in Red Deer or the mysterious sixth file we uncovered?" Tia inquired.

"No, we did not. There didn't seem to be much point," Sergeant Crombie replied.

"What about the Red Deer Rebel Kings connection? Are you planning to follow up on that?"

"That's up to the RCMP down there and they're not obliged to share any information with us. It may be time for us to close the case since we have identified the killer."

"But why did he kill them? How can you close the file without knowing that? What if it was a contract killing?"

"It's out of our jurisdiction. At this point, I don't see what more we can do," Sergeant Crombie replied. "But I understand your frustration. We certainly don't have a completely satisfactory answer."

The call ended then and Tia quickly arranged with Amanda to meet across the street at Roscoe's home where Claire and Roscoe were working together.

The three of them discussed the situation together while Roscoe went off to take a shower and get ready for his evening work at the restaurant.

Finally, Claire concluded, "If we want answers, one or more of us is going to have to go down there to check it out."

I'm not going!" Amanda declared. "Not after what happened to you and Gus. Those motorcycle gang types are obviously not people to fool around with."

Tia looked at Claire and shook her head apologetically. "I can't go either, Claire. Jimmy would have such a fit—and I can't even justify it on the grounds of personal freedom because there's the baby to consider."

"Well, I'll just have to go on my own, then," Claire concluded.

"No!" Tia said. "Too dangerous!"

Amanda looked at Claire thoughtfully. "If he agrees, you could take Matthew, as long as you do like last time and leave him out of the action and in a position to call for help if needed."

"I could do that," Claire acknowledged. Although obviously disappointed by the reaction of her two friends, this would be at least a way to make it possible.

Chapter 40: The Unexpected and a New Lead

Saturday morning saw Matthew and Claire driving down 50th Street in Red Deer at 11:30 in the morning. "Stop at that Tim Hortons," Claire instructed Matthew, who was driving. I need a coffee."

"Is yours empty already?" he asked, staring judgmentally at her large portable mug.

"Just do it, please," she responded. "And I also need a donut just in case."

Fifteen minutes later, Claire walked up the front steps of a modest home in the Southeast part of Red Deer alone. Matthew was parked across the street and several houses down. Both of their phone numbers were on speed dial. She rang the bell and nervously wiped the sugar from the donut off her lips.

"Yes, what do you want?" a harried-looking woman in her 40's inquired, as she opened the door.

"Does Mike Miller live here?" Claire asked.

"He's my son. Who are you?"

"I'm an investigator working in collaboration with the Edmonton Police Department. I'm following up on the recent death of your son's friend, Fil Deijers."

The woman looked alarmed and Claire hastily added, "Your son had nothing to do with that, but we are hoping that Fil might have shared some information with him that could help us to understand how the incident took place."

"Was he killed by that gang?" the woman asked, and Claire could see the fear in her eyes.

"The motorcycle gang, you mean?" Claire asked. The woman nodded her head mutely. "No, no! Nothing to do with that," Claire assured her. "We just need to talk to your son in case he knows anything about Fil that could help us understand what happened to him. That's why I'm here instead of the police. We don't want to involve him in an official police investigation unnecessarily."

Just then Claire noticed that a young man had come up behind the woman and now he said, "I'll take it from here, Mom. Don't worry."

The woman silently withdrew and Mike Miller led Claire into the living room. "What can I do to help?" he asked. "I don't understand what happened. It makes no sense to me. Fil was a good driver."

"First of all, thanks for agreeing to talk to me," Claire said. Her phone beeped then and she glanced at it, noting it was a text from Matthew. "I'm fine," she texted back and then gave her full attention to Mike. "Have you had a chance to hear all the details of the accident?"

"No," he replied. "Only what was reported on the news."

Claire told him then, even the bit about the crash helmet. Mike looked shocked. "Can you tell me any reason why Fil would have deliberately run into those people?"

"No-o," he said slowly. But after a pause, he added, "There was one thing. I don't know if it is related or not."

"What?" Claire asked encouragingly.

"Well, I know that Fil was really hoping to become a full patch member of the Hell's Angels in Edmonton but that usually means doing some dirty work for them beforehand."

"What kind of work?"

"Oh, just stuff. I don't know."

"How about you, Mike. Why did you join a motorcycle club?"

"I don't know. It's kind of cool belonging to a group like that. You always feel like somebody has your back. And I've always liked bikes."

"Well, do you have to do any of that kind of dirty work to belong to your club here?"

"Nah. It's just a social club really. It's only if you want to go deeper that. But most of the guys here—they just like the bang of roaring around on their bikes in a group. And it's a real chick magnet, too!"

"So how is it that you hooked up with Fil, then?"

Mike looked at her suspiciously. "How do you even know that? Why did you come here?"

"Well, there's one thing I haven't told you yet. Two things, actually. The guy who was killed was Gary Boaz, your accountant." Mike raised his eyebrows involuntarily. "We were able to crack into the hidden files on his computer and one of those files was about transferring some money offshore for you."

Mike looked quickly towards the door of the living room, checking to make sure his mother hadn't overheard this last statement. He hung his head and then he muttered, "It was a one-off. The Hells wanted help with a big heist last year. Fil and I agreed to assist them. I was just the driver but my share was 30 thou. The cops here are watching the banks for big, unexplained deposits and I didn't want my mother to know."

"Yes, but how did you meet Gary in the first place?"

"He's my dad's cousin. My parents divorced when I was seven but I still see my dad from time to time and a couple of times Gary was there when I visited. My dad once told me that Gary didn't always color within the lines so when I had this problem, I contacted him and he agreed to look after it for me."

"And Fil? What about him?"

"Fil is from Barbados and he has a mother and two younger sisters there. He wanted to send the money there so I put him in touch with Gary. We decided that we'd get Gary to send mine to Barbados, too."

Claire thought for a minute and then made a decision to reveal the other connection. "There were three files on Gary's computer from Hell's Angels in Edmonton—but that money went to Jamaica. Did you put them in touch with Gary, too?"

"Yes. In fact, that's why I got the $30,000.00. Fil only got 20. And he was one of the hold-up crew and actually shot one of the guards!"

"Did the guard die?" Claire asked, alarmed.

Mike looked scared, suddenly realizing that he'd been way too open with this total stranger. What will she do with this information? *I could be in trouble here!* he thought.

Claire saw the look and hastily added. "Look! I'm not interested in blabbing all this to the police. And whatever Fil did or didn't do, he's dead and can't be held accountable. All I want to do is to find out why Fil deliberately killed Gary—because there's no doubt that that's what happened. Do you think somebody in the Hell's Angels contracted him to do it?"

"Why?" Mike asked. "Those guys were really pleased to find someone who could take care of their money for them. It's not like Gary was trying to stiff them or anything—not that I know of, anyway."

"Why did they want their money to go to Jamaica? Why not Barbados, like you and Fil?"

"Jerry's from Jamaica and he knows the banking system there. He has contacts who could keep an eye on things if necessary. I guess they felt more comfortable doing that."

"Where are the others from?"

"Ron's family is originally from Quebec but they've been in Edmonton quite a while. Bennie's from Mexico but he didn't want anything to do with sending money there. The whole system is corrupt," he said. "He figured he might lose it that way."

"What's the relationship between your club here and the Hell's Angels in Edmonton?"

"We're like their gophers. If they want a job done but don't want to get their hands dirty then they call us."

"And what's in it for you guys?"

"Quick money—but also, that's the only way to prove that any of us are mean enough and tough enough to be considered for the Hells. Joining up with them is the big goal of a lot of our guys."

"And how about you?"

"Nah. I feel bad enough already. After Fil shot that guy I just wanted to get out of it all."

"That's not so easy, I understand. Would the Rebel Kings let you out?"

"Our club is kind of loose compared to the Hells. And we're small potatoes as far as they're concerned. "I'm just going to move away and that should deal with that. I got admitted to the University of Saskatchewan and I'm going to start there in the fall—in the business faculty."

"But what are you going to do until then?"

"I'm leaving next week but I'm not talking about it. I have enough money to get settled and I'm going to work on getting my money back from Barbados. I don't quite know how to do that, though, now that Gary's gone."

"My aunt and her soon-to-be new husband will be there in a few days. They're on a cruise and are getting married in Barbados. Her fiancée is a member of Gary's firm so if you gave me the information to pass onto him I'm sure he could arrange something for you."

Mike looked very happy when he heard this and he and Claire talked some more about the money that was in Barbados.

Chapter 41: A Wedding, an Argument and a Challenge

Gus found it very exciting at first to be on a cruise ship. It was a new experience for her. She walked all over the four levels, checking out the shopping, the pool and the games room. Gus carefully avoided the various food and drink amenities, as she didn't want to be tempted and put on weight. She enjoyed reading a mystery book on the private balcony of their 450-square foot ocean view suite and spent a lot of time talking to John. They had much yet to learn about each other.

After two days of this, Gus was restless, though, and began researching the Rebel Kings' motorcycle club on her computer. John, in the meantime, was working on the wedding arrangements. By good fortune, he had a friend in Barbados, a former classmate. Randy Gosling and his wife, Althea, had been thrilled to hear the happy news and had insisted on handling all the details for the wedding.

John spent a lot of time emailing back and forth with his friend in order to finalize the plans while Gus remained strangely disinterested, leaving it mostly up to him. She felt little enthusiasm for putting much effort into a wedding that nobody important to her other than John would be there to witness.

But in large part, her lack of interest was because she was preoccupied about fulfilling the commitment she'd made to Claire to retrieve the money from the bank accounts of both Fil and Mike. It had turned out that Mike might know more than he'd initially let on, and this was his condition for sharing it with Claire.

On the third day, they docked in Bridgetown, Barbados, at seven in the morning.

They were scheduled to be there that day anyway, but the ship's engineer had identified a serious problem with the engine the day before. They had sailed all night at half speed in order to get there before the engine gave out entirely. He wouldn't know what parts would be required for repairs until the ship was docked and he could examine the engine properly without risking stranding them in the middle of the ocean.

Before arrival, the passengers were warned that they must take all their personal belongings with them when they disembarked because it would be necessary for them to change ships. Rooms had been arranged for them in the local Hilton Hotel for the day and a sister cruise ship was on its way to replace their ship. They would board it at eight that night and were given the docking stall number.

John's friends met Gus and John at the terminal and looked surprised when they saw them lugging their suitcases. The timeline for the ten o'clock wedding was tight but they whisked them quickly away to their hotel when they heard what had happened to the ship. John registered and the four of them trooped up to the suite they'd been assigned, carting the bags with them. John and Gus were already decked out in their wedding clothes, having decided it was better to look a bit odd getting off the ship then to have to rush later to get ready in time. So as soon as they dumped off the bags, the four of them left.

They rode to the wedding site in Randy's BMW hybrid and Gus privately thought it even more comfortable and luxurious than John's Mercedes. The drive was about half an hour and along the way, they picked up the minister who was to perform the ceremony. He was unconventional looking to say the least and Gus threw furtive glances at his dreadlocks, beads, long gown and sandals. Finally, she couldn't keep quiet any longer. "Are you a Rastafarian?" she asked.

The others laughed and Minister McFadden replied, "No. I grew up in the Kirk, The Church of Scotland, and that's where I was ordained. But I've been here for ten years now and island life is different. This is a beach wedding and I've adapted my style to suit."

Gus didn't look convinced but John squeezed her hand and gave her a reassuring look. Soon they were there—at a deserted beach, with only the seagulls for an audience. Gus looked in dismay at her delicate silver pumps, and Althea reached over and patted her arm. "People do these beach weddings in bare feet, Gus," she said, reaching down to remove her own shoes.

They then walked/waded across the soft, white sand towards the small canopy near the water where the ceremony would take place. Strangely, neither Gus nor John had thought much about the actual ceremony itself. So much had been happening. All they both knew for sure was that they wanted to be together. Now, lined up in front of this unlikely-looking minister with Althea at her side and Randy beside John, Gus was suddenly struck by how surreal and anticlimactic the whole thing was. Somehow they stumbled through their vows, exchanged the obligatory kiss and then waded through the sand to where a small table had been set up. A couple of the local ladies made a business out of organizing brunches to follow these morning weddings.

Ian Mcfadden, Randy and Althea toasted John and Gus with a rum cocktail and then they all shared the seafood soup followed by poached flying fish and cou cou (a Barbadian staple made with okra and cornmeal). This was accompanied by various salads and fresh island fruits and followed by an exotic pineapple-coconut cake. After they finished eating, Gus pulled a large Ziploc food bag out of her purse and placed the remains of the cake inside. She turned to the others with an apologetic look. "I promised to bring some of the wedding cake back to my friends in Edmonton so they could share a little in our ceremony," she said. The others nodded understandingly.

Soon it was time to leave for the drive back to the hotel and along the way Randy dropped the minister off at his home. Gus noted that it had a modern, comfortable and definitely happy look to it. His wife, a tall, attractive, Black woman, met him at the door with a gentle embrace. Gus was finally convinced that Reverend Ian McFadden was indeed a real minister and that she and John were now really married. When they reached the hotel, Randy and Althea declined their invitation to come in for a drink and arranged to meet them later that afternoon to drive them back to the ship.

Back in their hotel room, John turned to take Gus in his arms. But after a brief embrace, she moved away and sat down in one of the two comfortable armchairs that had been provided. He sat down in the other and looked at her quizzically. "What's wrong, Gustava?"

"I'm sorry. I know this is our wedding day and we should be all romantic right now but it's like we've already had our honeymoon this past ten days and it's been wonderful. But now I have things on my mind."

"About us?" he asked guardedly.

"No-o-o," she sighed, not sure if she should say more.

"Come on, spit it out!"

"It's just that I made a promise…"

"Yes, you did—a couple of hours ago on the beach."

"Not that promise—although that's part of it."

"Go on," he said patiently.

"Well, you agreed you'd go to the bank this afternoon and make good Claire's offer to transfer Mike's money back to that bank account he set up in Saskatoon so he could pay for his university tuition there—and we board the ship at eight tonight."

"Yes, I did agree—and we'll have plenty of time to do that later this afternoon. It's a very simple, straightforward process, and Randy told me that the Trident bank stays open until six. He also deals there"

"Yes, but that's not all."

"What?" he asked, no longer sounding so patient.

"I promised Claire something—and you may not like it ... but it has to be done."

"What?"

"The guy who died, Fil, left his ID with Mike and made him promise that if something happened to him Mike would make sure that his family here in Barbados got the money in his account in that bank."

"Why would you want to help with that?" John asked, anticipating what Gus was about to ask him. "He's the person who deliberately killed Gary and Marion."

"Because Mike told Claire that he knows what happened, why Fil killed them. But he's not going to tell her the story unless she makes sure this is done while I'm here so he can keep his promise to Fil."

"And how do you propose to do that? The bank is not going to turn over the money to anyone other that the depositor. The only reason I can transfer Mike's money is because it's going back into an account in his name."

"Do you remember when you had your nap yesterday afternoon on the boat? Well, I took the opportunity to contact Fil's brother. He lives in Bridgetown with his mother and two younger half-sisters. There's no father in the picture."

John said nothing but raised his eyebrows.

"Anyway," Gus went on. "From the picture of him Fil gave to Mike that I now have along with Mike's ID, they look a lot alike. I'm hoping he can just walk into the bank with the ID and get the money. I arranged to meet him here at 1:30 to pass on the ID and discuss the details with him for getting the money." Gus gulped and looked at John to see how he was reacting.

John just looked back at her and said nothing at first. Finally, he commented, "And when were you going to tell me about your private plans on how to spend our wedding day?"

"This seemed like a good time," Gus said lamely.

John got up. "I think I'm going to go for a walk," he said somewhat tersely. He went into the bedroom, changed into casual clothes and then walked out the door. "I'll see you later," was all he said as he left.

Gus felt numb and dully sad at the same time. For a few minutes she couldn't think what to do. But then she checked her watch and saw that it was already 1:15 so she quickly changed and went downstairs to the lobby.

Chapter 42: The Impossible Becomes Possible

Gus recognized Fil's brother immediately when he entered the lobby. He did look strikingly like Fil from what Gus could tell from the driver's license picture. As he walked tentatively towards her, Gus looked for signs of arrogance or a general air of anti-socialness. After all, this family had bred a killer. But she saw nothing unusual.

"Are you Gus?" he asked. She nodded and he sat down.

"I'm Fil's brother, Jason."

Now that he was sitting only two feet away from her across the small table that separated them, Gus could see how young he looked and began to worry. "How old are you?" she asked.

"Seventeen," he replied.

"Are you still in school?"

"Yes, grade eleven. I was thinking I'd have to drop out now that Fil is gone and get a job. He used to send money home every month and that was all that kept us going. But now maybe—is it really $20,000.00 like you say?" Gus nodded. "That would keep us going for a long time. I could even finish grade twelve. And maybe then I could gradually do the Optician's diploma course on-line while I worked and then do my practicum hours with one of our local opticians so I could get licensed!"

"Sounds like you've been looking into it. Why are you so interested in becoming an optician?"

"Well, I'd really like to become an optometrist or ophthalmologist but that takes way too long and costs a pile. My mom has retinal detachment and she's almost blind. That's why she can't work any longer and we needed help from Fil all the time."

"Oh, I'm sorry to hear that. What kind of work did she do?"

"She was a seamstress but then when her eyes got bad she couldn't do that any longer so she started taking in washing. But now she can't even do that because she can't see the stains on the clothes well enough to clean them and people were complaining and didn't hire her anymore."

"I'm sorry to hear that," Gus said. To herself she added, *Fil's family really needs this money and I'm going to make it happen, whatever John thinks!* Gus turned to Jason again and went on. "I don't have much time. Our ship leaves at eight. We better get to work!"

"I'm ready," he said.

"No, you're not. You don't look anything like your brother with that long hair and sloppy island clothing!" Jason looked offended but Gus hastily went on. "There's a lot at stake here. Are you prepared to do what's necessary?"

"I don't have money for fancy clothes like Fil wore."

"Don't worry. "I'll take care of that. But first you need to come upstairs with me so I can cut your hair. Fil's hair was short."

"No way! It's taken me years to grow my hair out like this!" Jason objected.

"The date on Fil's driver's license renewal is only six months ago. Your hair can be a little longer than his but not much, maybe an inch or two."

A variety of emotions flitted across Jason's face: horror, sadness and finally resignation. He rose meekly and went with Gus up to her room. All the way up in the elevator, she was reviewing in her mind whether or not she'd brought her barber shears. John had been taken aback by the size of her suitcase but Gus didn't travel much and had not known what to bring. Therefore, she'd just brought everything she thought she might possibly need. And when, back in the room, she opened her cosmetics case, there they were!

Gus wrapped a towel around Jason's neck, tied it with a safety pin she'd also brought along in case she needed it and got to work. First she braided his hair into one long queue and then clipped it off. She placed the braid on a clean hand towel so he could take it home with him and then began shaping his hair in as close an approximation of Fil's cut as she could manage. But, just as she was finishing up the final touches, the room door opened and John walked into the bathroom.

"What's going on?" he asked sharply. But then he saw the driver's license that Gus had kept on the counter to consult while she was styling Jason's hair. "I see-e-e," he said slowly. He looked at Jason's clothing and asked, "You're not going to try going to the bank dressed like that, are you?"

"No, I don't think so," Jason stuttered.

"I'll go shopping for you—but I wish we had a measuring tape."

"Just a minute!" Gus said and when she returned to the bathroom, she was triumphantly holding a tape.

"What made you think you'd need to bring that along?" John asked her, a note of amusement in his voice.

"I thought I might like to buy something to wear since I didn't have time to shop before we left and I wasn't sure if every place had dressing rooms."

"Hmm, good call! Well, get out of here now so I can measure this guy up but bring me a pen and some paper first."

When Gus returned with the required items, she heard John asking Jason, "Which side do you dress on?" She didn't want to know what that meant and hurriedly scurried away.

While John was out purchasing the necessary items, Jason had a quick shower, wrapped himself in the guest dressing gown and put on the slippers provided by the hotel. Fortunately, there was a complimentary toothbrush and toothpaste neither Gus nor John had needed so he was able to attend to that matter as well. Gus then handed him a razor with a new blade and some shaving cream, also from her personal supply kit. While he shaved, Gus did her best to clean and shine his sandals with the complimentary shoeshine cloth but the results were not impressive.

Soon John was back. He'd taken the measurements, studied the picture and, most importantly, talked to Jason about what Fil was like so the clothing selections he'd settled on looked quite credible. Once Jason was dressed, he looked very different but it was still quite evident that he was a teenager. Gus took him back to the bathroom and skillfully applied make-up to age his appearance. "How did you do that?" John asked in surprise when they emerged.

"I was always interested in theatre and originally I'd hoped to be an actor. That's why I chose to do a Theatre Arts degree. And part of my training was make-up application for character actors, making them look older or younger or more or less attractive." She turned to Jason then. "Just remember not to touch your face or get too close to them so they can see the make-up." Jason nodded.

Chapter 43: It's Now or Never!

After Jason had been made to look as much like Fil as possible, John motioned for him to sit down in the living room. "Looking the part is one thing, but acting it is another!" Drawing on his many years of work in the investment world, John rehearsed various possible scenarios with Jason, playing the role of the bank manager or employee. It took a good half hour but finally Jason was able to make his request to withdraw the money from Fil's account, implying that it was his own, and to handle any likely questions that might be thrown his way quickly and smoothly.

In the interim, Gus busied herself cleaning up the bathroom to remove any evidence of their unregistered guest. She was feeling increasingly nervous and called out, "John, it's already past three and we don't know how long the banks are open!"

"Don't worry," he called back. "Trident is open until six and we're just finishing. I transferred Mike's money when I was out this morning. It took less than 15 minutes. We'll go back there now and see if this ruse will work to get Fil's money out!"

Gus came into the living room then and listened to Jason run through his lines one last time with John playing the role of bank employee or manager and Jason explaining to him that he needed to close out *his* account. She was amazed at how much older and more sophisticated Jason sounded now than he had when she first met him. Clearly he was ready to play his part. However, Gus had one question.

"What are you going to do with all that cash?"

John and Jason looked at each other and then Jason stuttered "I don't know."

"You can't walk around with it—and it's not a very good idea to just hide it under the mattress. What if there was a fire?"

"But you also can't transfer it to another bank because then you'd have to transfer it in Fil's name," John said. He was mentally kicking himself for not having thought about this problem earlier.

"Could you put it in a bank near your home?" Gus asked. "Maybe tell them you won it in a lottery or something?"

"They know me there and they'd notice how I'd changed my appearance and get suspicious. And don't lotteries usually give you checks?"

Gus thought for a minute and then said, "I have an idea. Go to a bank a little further away from your home where nobody knows you—and not a branch of Trident just in case. Say the money came from the sale of a recreational vehicle you owned and the owner wanted to pay you in cash for some reason. You were anxious to sell it. You'd been trying for a long time—and you didn't want to argue."

"Sounds plausible," John agreed.

"Okay, I can do that," Jason agreed. "Recreational vehicle," he muttered to himself. He got up, ready to go.

"Just a minute!" Gus said. She hurriedly consulted the internet via her new computer and five minutes later turned to him. "If anyone asks you what RV you're selling, just say it's a Four Winds Majestic. If they ask about brand say Ford. If they ask what type say Class C. And if they ask about size say 25 feet. If they ask about a cab over say no. Don't volunteer any information and don't sound patient giving responses or offer any elaboration. Act like you're in a hurry and have things to do." As she said this, Gus was typing it out. She was an expert typist after all her office experience. She then pulled a portable micro-printer out of her suitcase and quickly printed a copy. "Here! Study this in the car. If they ask something you're not sure of just say, 'I forget.'"

John looked amazed. "What on earth were you doing carrying a printer along on a cruise?"

"You never know when you might need one," Gus replied.

"But they always have a whole office on these cruise ships—computers, fax machines and printers that clients can access."

"Well, I didn't know that, did I? I've never been on a cruise before."

"Good thing, too!" Jason muttered, with his head down while he frantically rehearsed the new information Gus had prepared for him.

John just shook his head and smirked. Then he said, "We'd better get going. I rented a car while I was out. It's a dark blue Buick Challenger and I'll park across the street from the bank and wait for you there. As soon as you have the money, come out and get in the car and we'll leave quickly—just in case anybody gets suspicious. Then we'll drive directly to the other bank. "I'll wait for you outside and then drive you home and then I'll turn in the car and go back to the hotel."

"What about me?" Gus asked.

"Gus, you pack up while we're gone and get the porter to take the bags downstairs to the checkroom. Then wait in the lobby for Randy and Althea. They're meeting us there at 5:00 for dinner and a last visit and then they're going to drive us to the ship. Just tell them there were complications with the business transaction I had to complete and I'll be late. Do not say anything about what's really happening!"

Later, at ten that night, John and Gus were lying in bed talking. Both of them were exhausted and could hardly keep their eyes open.

"I can't believe we pulled it off," Gus commented.

"It was touch and go there for awhile. Jason told me that the bank manager was called in and he clearly was suspicious. He wanted Jason to stay longer. Gave him some story about checking out a bank for him to transfer the money to. But Jason just left and I saw both the manager and the teller peering out the window at the car."

"Do you think they got the license number or recognized that it was from the rental agency?" Gus asked, concerned.

"Actually, after I rented the car, I purchased a removable decal and stuck it over the rental decal on the car. I also stuck bits of gray putty on the license plate to look like mud splatters and obscure some of the numbers. And after Jason deposited most of the money in the other bank, I took him to the bus stop instead of driving him home. Then I parked the car, got rid of the decal and the putty and then returned the car to the rental agency and took a cab back to the hotel. That's why I was able to get there by six and have supper with you and Randy and Althea."

"This couldn't have happened without your help, John. Why did you do it? You seemed so angry when you left for your walk in the afternoon!"

"I was angry. It seemed like you considered everything and everybody else more important than our wedding and me. But as I walked, I realized something. Your life has been turned upside down. I can't expect to just walk back into it and take over. I can't tell you what to think or feel or prioritize."

"I haven't even had a chance to tell you what Jason told me about him and his family yet, John. Maybe then you'll understand why it was so important to me."

After Gus told him the story, John looked at her fondly. "I guess you were doing the right thing then, Gustava," he replied, "and I'm glad I could help."

"You more than helped! I can't believe how sneaky and clever you were about it all. I'm sure when I tell the others, they'll want to make you an honorary member of our team!"

Goody! John muttered to himself. And a few seconds later they were both sound asleep. Their *wedding night* had to wait for the morning.

Chapter 44: Back to the Honeymoon

It was eleven the next morning by the time Gus and John managed to stumble to the restaurant for breakfast but they discovered it was closed and they had to make do with what they could find at the espresso bar. This was unfortunate because they were both very hungry. With all the excitement of the day before they hadn't eaten much and that combined with their earlier morning activities had left them in strong need of nourishment.

Over cups of double strength cappuccino, bagels laden with cream cheese and lox and a tired-looking collection of cut fruit, they discussed their plans for the rest of the day. "I must contact Claire and tell her mission accomplished!" Gus said.

We can use the computer in the ship's tourist office, scan in the receipt Jason gave me as well as the one I got for transferring Mike's money, and you can send them to Claire as email attachments. That way Claire can contact Mike right away and tell him she's bringing the proof that his wishes were carried out. You might know by the end of the day who was behind the killing!"

"That's great!" Gus exclaimed. "I can't believe how far technology has come since the days of the electronic typewriters I worked with!"

"It is pretty amazing," John agreed.

After their breakfast, they returned to their room to pick up the receipts and then located the tourist office. Gus sent the message to Claire with John's help to scan in the receipts and attach them. Then they went for a stroll around this new ship to see if it was any different than the previous one. Eventually they settled in deck chairs on the top deck, Gus still holding onto her new laptop. She'd insisted on bringing it with her to the tourist office in case the one there didn't work.

It was two in the afternoon and somehow they'd managed to miss the formal lunch as well as the formal breakfast. They asked the bar attendant for sandwiches and cruised around the salad bar set up there at lunchtime. After eating, Gus thought she should check her computer again. Claire had sent a response:

That's great news, Aunt Gus. Quite a coup! I'm looking forward to hearing all the details when you get back. I phoned Mike but there was no answer. If there are any developments, I'll let you know. Now relax and enjoy the rest of your honeymoon! Hello to John.
Love,
Claire

In the remaining three days of their trip, Gus didn't hear anything further from Claire but she didn't mind. She and John were continuing the process of getting acquainted with who they were at this point in their respective lives and discovering new interests that they could share together. They attended a couple of presentations on oceanography as well as a cooking lesson from the sous-chef, who happened to be Northern Italian, on how to make gnocchi. They found they didn't enjoy playing cards with another older couple that obviously spent a lot of their time engaged in that activity. But they did enjoy quietly working on crossword puzzles together. Gus had neither the interest nor mathematical bent to match John's facility with Sudoku. "Why does the world have to keep changing all the time?" Gus grumbled. And John just smiled at her fondly.

Chapter 45: Was All That For Nothing?

Back in Edmonton, Claire finally got an answer on the home phone where Mike lived with his mother. "Hello," came the answer, in a dull voice. "Mary Miller speaking."

A premonitory chill down ran down Claire's back. She gave her name and asked to speak to Mike. "I've phoned a couple of times," she added, "but nobody was home."

"I was in Edmonton," Mary replied flatly. "With Mike."

"Oh-h—Mike is in Edmonton now?"

"At the Royal Alec—in intensive care."

Claire gasped. "What happened?"

"Those motorcycle guys. They beat him up. He's in a coma."

Claire could not respond immediately. She hardly knew what to say. Finally, she reached a decision. Whatever promise of confidentiality she'd made to Mike seemed moot at this point. "Mary, I don't know what to say. I had some good news for Mike and I know some things. May I come and see you, please, so I can tell you?"

There was silence at the other end of the line. Finally, Mary spoke. "Come. I need to know. Why did they do this to my son? Why?"

"I'm leaving now—as soon as I can get some things in place. I should be there in two hours. Is that okay?"

Claire heard a sob at the other end of the line and then a single word—"come"—and the phone went dead.

Claire hastily made arrangements for coverage at Roscoe's home and her own home and was on the road in twenty minutes. She was not one to overthink things!

When she arrived at Mike's home, Mary opened the door and Claire spontaneously threw her arms around her. Mary led her to the living room and told the following story. Mike had gone to the gym for a workout three days earlier. When he came out at about eight in the evening, three guys on motorcycles ran him down and took turns beating him according to a couple of passers-by. Fortunately, a police cruiser drove by a few minutes later and scared them off but Mike had taken a severe blow to the head and was now in critical condition on life support. All the police heard when they jumped out of the car was those guys calling out, "You shouldn't have tried to leave. You made a vow."

"It's not clear whether or not Mike will ever recover or even if he'll live. I don't know how they found out about his plan to move to Saskatoon. I certainly never told anyone," Mary said. Then she looked at Claire suspiciously. "Did you?"

"No! Well, yes—but no. I only told my aunt because I needed to—and she had to tell her husband." And Claire then told Mary the story about the money and how John had managed to get it transferred back in Mike's name to a bank near the University of Saskatchewan.

Mary was shocked but then she said, "I know he really wanted to go to university but couldn't figure how to get enough money for the tuition. And what you say about him not wanting any more to do with them after the guard was hurt ... that sounds like Mike. He was never mean like that! He was basically on the soft side. I wish to God he'd never gotten involved with those punks!"

Claire just looked at her. "What are the doctors saying? Will he recover?"

"They don't know. They say every case is different. He may not live. And if he does..." Mary stopped talking to choke back a sob.

"What?" Claire asked, somewhat insensitively, but she needed to know.

"Brain damage!" Mary gasped. "He's likely to have brain damage!" All that risk to get the money for university and it's not even going to happen now. It was all for nothing!"

Claire didn't know what to say. She felt sick. "May I visit him?" she asked in a weak voice.

"If you like and if they let you in," Mary responded dully. "But there's nothing to see. He just lies there breathing through a machine with a blank look on his face like there's nobody home." She cried then and Claire tried to comfort her but she couldn't think of any words to say that would have been of the slightest use.

Shortly after, Claire left for home. She felt aimless and disoriented and stopped at the nearest Tim Horton's for coffee and the largest apple fritter they had in their tray. She sought out a small booth at the very back of the coffee shop. When she finished her donut and had wiped her fingers, she called Tia, looking around carefully first to make sure no one could overhear her. In terse words and using as many general terms as possible, she explained what had happened, all the time searching her immediate environment to make sure no one could hear. Tia responded predictably and asked Claire to stop by and tell her in more detail on her way home.

After she hung up the phone, Claire knew she felt strong enough to drive now. She'd needed to hear Tia's outrage and to feel Tia's pain. Sharing the pain somehow made it more bearable. Selfish maybe—but necessary in this case.

When she arrived at Tia's house, Jimmy opened the door and for once he didn't look annoyed to see her. He was usually very protective of Tia and jealous of her attention to others, particularly Claire. But this time, she actually saw a look of compassion on his face and he motioned her towards the living room where Tia was waiting for her.

They sat together numbly for a couple of minutes just looking at each other and realizing how important it was to be together at that moment. Finally, Claire said, "I keep thinking that maybe it's my fault. If I hadn't gone there? Maybe one of them saw me? Maybe they thought he was a snitch?"

"But that's not what the police heard them saying, according to what you told me."

"I know—but I can't get it out of my head."

"In any case, it's not about you!" Tia said rather harshly. "What can we do to help him—or his mother? And how are we going to track down those bastards? I gather they got away?"

"Can you call Sergeant Crombie? You said he had a contact there. Maybe he can at least find out what they know or who they suspect and we'd have something to go on."

"I'll try," Tia agreed. "It'll be better than doing nothing."

"Let's not tell the others right now," Claire requested. "We certainly don't want Aunt Gus to know. Let her have the couple of days left of her honeymoon uncluttered by all this mess. She did enough!"

"I agree," Tia said. "It's best we just keep it to ourselves until she gets back. It's only three more days anyway."

They left it at that and Claire went home to attend to her domestic duties. But the sick feeling remained in her stomach the rest of the evening and returned to haunt her the next day.

Chapter 46: Back on Track

Gus and John returned from their honeymoon cruise on Sunday. They docked at Miami at noon, caught a three o'clock flight back to Edmonton and were home and in bed by eleven that evening. Claire gave them a day to get organized and then arranged a meeting at Amanda's house for Tuesday at seven. She had Amanda make the calls and said nothing about what had happened to Mike. She still felt sick about it. And on Sunday afternoon she had visited him. He'd been moved to a private room but was still in a coma. However, he was breathing on his own.

Both Gus and John turned up at Amanda's house shortly after seven. He declared that he wanted to be a part of the team and nobody objected. In fact, the others were delighted to see him. Also present were Hilda, Hilda's dog Job, Matthew, Claire, Tia, and, of course, Amanda. Gus raised her eyebrows when she saw the dog. Tia quietly took her aside and explained that Hilda had become agoraphobic since her double loss and it was hard for her to go anywhere. Having Job along made it easier and they definitely needed her at this meeting.

When the meeting started, Claire asked Gus and John to go first. The two of them described in detail and with a certain amount of relish the various events that had taken place during their highly compressed day in Barbados. John finished by saying, "Mike should be able to easily access the money from the Saskatoon bank when he gets there. Did he leave already?"

This was Claire's cue. She glanced briefly at Tia and then turned to the rest of them with a sober look on her face. "Mike is in hospital in a coma. He was badly beaten a week ago by several of his fellow gang members. Apparently, they found out he was planning to leave." Claire watched the happy, eager look on the face of her Aunt Gus crumble into sorrow and she felt sick all over once again.

"Why didn't you tell us sooner?" John asked. Gus added, "After all we did!"

"I only found out the day after your email, Aunt Gus—and I didn't want to ruin the rest of your honeymoon. Claire turned to the rest of the group now and added, "I told Tia but we wanted to get more details before sharing this horrible news with the rest of you. Tia has been in touch with Sergeant Crombie and has learned something." She motioned to Tia who took over the floor and Claire sank back into her chair gratefully.

"We found …" Tia stopped because she saw the gray look on Hilda's face and noted that she was weaving a bit in the hard-backed chair in which she was seated. Job was licking her hand but it wasn't enough. Everyone was looking at her now. Amanda got up and led Hilda to the armchair where Matthew was and he quickly jumped out. Amanda sat Hilda down, put the footrest up and put a blanket over her knees.

Gus had been holding Waldorf. He and Salatta were staying with Amanda for the time being. Gus went over to Hilda now and placed Waldorf in her lap. Hilda picked him up and held her face against him for a minute and, for some reason, Waldorf tolerated it. Then she put him back down on her lap. He curled up and she coiled one hand around him while placing her other hand back on Job's head.

"I feel better now," she rasped. "Thanks."

Nobody said anything but there was a palpable sense in the room that they all had suddenly realized how fragile life is.

"We'll all have to be careful," Amanda said, echoing this feeling. This case is different than all the other ones we've worked on. We need to find the person responsible for killing Gary and Marion. We need to do this for Hilda's sake. But the timeline is not as urgent as it was in all those other cases. We can afford to go slow and be cautious."

Several heads nodded and Tia carried on. "I talked to Sergeant Crombie Friday morning and he promised to check with his friend, Jack Wrigby, in Red Deer. This morning he called me back. Apparently, the RCMP officers on the case were able to track down one of the three perpetrators a short time after it happened, a 17-year-old named Steve Larson. They checked him over at the station and the lab results showed he had Mike's blood under his fingernails so there was no question he was involved.

Once they heard back from the hospital that Mike's condition was critical, they told Steve he might be facing a murder charge. After that, he cracked pretty easily and gave up the names of the other two. They were picked up and an identity parade was organized. There were a couple of witnesses to the attack and they were able to pick them out of the line-up. All three are in jail now, charged with assault and attempt to commit murder, and their first court appearance is this coming Friday."

"But why did they do it? Were they after the money?" Gus asked.

"I couldn't say anything to Sergeant Crombie about the money, could I?"

"Oh, yes. That's right," Gus remembered.

"Did the three of them have any dealings with Gary?" Hilda wanted to know.

"They were asked that at Inspector McCoy's request. Sergeant Crombie told him what had happened. But none of them admitted to knowing Gary and there's nothing on his computer to connect them to him."

"So this likely doesn't tie in with Gary's and Marion's deaths then," Hilda said.

"No-o, it doesn't seem to," Claire acknowledged.

"Well, where do we go from here?" John asked, a bit impatiently.

"Matthew?" Tia said.

Matthew got up and stood in front of them and Tia sat down. "I've been following up on the sixth file we got off that memory stick in Gary's locker. Like Hilda said, it doesn't seem to be Gary's work. But it looks more and more like it *is* the work of somebody connected with the company. That's why it's good that you're here, John—but it's too bad we don't have Sean here as well….oh, I guess that wouldn't work, would it?" he said, with some embarrassment.

"No-o," John said evenly. "It's just as well that he *not* find out about the Barbados money transactions. Anyway, we talked to him quite extensively about the situation before this all happened and the only information he could give us over and above what you told us, Hilda, was that Gary and Dave Stout spent a lot of time in each other's offices with the doors closed. If you think that the sixth file was work out of our office then I think he's the most likely candidate—and Gary had a copy for some reason. But why are you so sure it's from our office? I'd like to see it."

"I have a copy right here," Matthew said, and handed it over.

John blanched reflexively at this casual handling of a confidential document. But he scanned it quickly and then said, "I see what you mean."

"Well, enlighten the rest of us, will you, please," Gus growled.

Tia looked at Claire and gave a quick grin.

"It's the format," John explained. Each investment company has its own signature style. Just a lot of little things like how the signature is spaced out, the standard greeting at the top. This is just a worksheet, of course, so those elements are missing but even the borders, where the page number is, the font. It all looks familiar."

"I knew there was something about it I recognized," Hilda muttered.

"Well, where do we go from here?" Gus asked. "Should I go in again and do my thing? I could tell your receptionist I'm not happy with Sean's work and I've heard good things about this Dave guy and would like to try him out."

"I'm afraid that wouldn't work," John smiled. "Your cover is shot."

"Why? What did you tell them?" Gus looked annoyed.

"Nothing, not a thing. Though I can't speak for Sean. But when an attractive woman comes in to meet with an investment counselor and remains behind a closed office door for 2½ hours and then leaves with the counselor's father, people will talk!"

"Oh," Gus said, somewhat mollified. The others snickered and she blushed.

Hilda cleared her throat preparatory to speaking. Waldorf jumped down and stalked away, annoyed by this disruption. She turned to Claire and Tia. "You remember I told you awhile ago I was hoping to have memorial celebrations for Gary and Marion? Well, Job and I finally went out to the crematorium and picked up the cremains the other day—and we also ordered the urns." She looked at Claire and Tia then and shook her head quickly, privately indicating to them that she'd not gone with the piggy bank idea after all.

"When are you hoping to have the service—or will there be two?" Tia asked.

"Soon, I hope. And there will only be one. I've decided that's all I can handle. But the reason I'm mentioning it now is that Dave Stout is sure to come and it would be an opportunity for you to meet him. I could get him to speak about how he knew Gary as part of the service. That might give you some idea of who he is."

"Could work," John said thoughtfully. "It gives us a starting point anyway."

"Okay with me," Claire added. "We don't really have anywhere else to go from here."

It was agreed. Hilda said she'd work with Tia and Claire to settle the details and get back to the rest of them once everything was in place. If all went well, they could have the service within the week. The others murmured sounds of approval and the meeting broke up shortly after that.

Chapter 47: Can Funerals Ever Be Fun?

True to her word, Hilda organized the dual memorial celebration for Gary and Marion for the following Tuesday afternoon at 3 p.m. That made it almost one month after the accident. Claire arranged for the services to be held in her church with her minister since Hilda had no church and the few times Marion had been able to get away on a Sunday without upsetting Hilda and Gary too much, she'd come along with Claire to her church. The reception was scheduled to follow in the church basement after the service and since it was going to be basically suppertime at that point it was set up as a buffet dinner.

Claire and Tia helped with all the technical arrangements and Amanda organized the flowers. Hilda met with the minister on two separate occasions, first to discuss what she chose to share about Gary and then to describe her mother and what she believed her mother's life had stood for. Both times, she handed the minister a written summary of the key points. Hilda didn't believe in trusting anything so important to memory.

John took care of the advertising. He acquired flattering pictures of Gary and Marion, got the necessary information about them from Hilda, prepared the death announcements and got her to make any desired changes. He put them in the newspaper for the five days prior to plus the day of the service, and he prepared a joint poster for the office with Gary and Marion's pictures side by side. He did not tell Hilda about this because he was fairly sure she wouldn't like it. His thinking was that the idea of a double memorial service might intrigue more people from the office to come out and that would provide more possible fodder for Claire and her group of trusty detectives. He also injected some extra cash into the buffet dinner to encourage people to stick around longer.

Claire and Tia rode with Hilda on the day of the funeral. They sat in the back seat with Bill and Hilda in the front. Bill was having a hard time understanding that Marion was really gone forever. He couldn't quite seem to grasp the concept and kept asking Claire over and over when she would come back. Claire hoped that the funeral service would help to give him closure. At the church, the four of them filed into the reserved front row. Hilda had no one else.

The minister stayed close to the script he'd been given in his remarks. He hadn't known Gary at all and had seen Marion only a few times in his church when she accompanied Claire. Personal remarks from friends were to be shared at the reception downstairs where the mourners were pleasantly surprised to see that wine was being served. John had also arranged for this. He thought it might help to loosen tongues.

John and Sean, as prearranged between them, made their way through the collection of mourners from Gary's workplace—nine in all—including Dave Stout and the office receptionist. Only three people were present from Hilda's workplace: her supervisor, Marlene Hastings, the office secretary, Carolyn Cohen, and her one friend, Jack Shaw. Hilda had not returned there since the accident.

The small group of friends who'd clustered around Bill and Mavis and Roscoe were the only people who were close to Marion. Roscoe was present with his parents and his Uncle Daisuke, but Mavis and Jessie were not present. Claire hadn't seen the point, particularly since there was important observational work to be done and she couldn't afford to be distracted.

Once the group of about 25 people had convened downstairs, Jimmy took over as MC. He spoke first about his own relationship with Marion, and how much he'd counted on her to keep him informed about his sister Mavis when she and Bill were both still in the institution in Calgary. He talked about her work on the parent committee there and how hard she'd tried to make a life for Bill here in Edmonton. He tried to make some consoling remarks about how close she'd been to Hilda but it didn't quite ring true for those who'd known them and witnessed their relationship. Claire, sitting next to Hilda, saw her drop her head and watched as a couple of tears fell.

Sean spoke next, recalling his university days with Gary and relating an amusing incident or two. He remembered him as a loving husband and someone who was very competent at his job. Again, it didn't ring quite true. After he finished, Dave got up to speak. It was obvious that he'd had the opportunity to dip into the wine at that point. His face was flushed and his remarks were rather longer than necessary. He spoke about their joint love of racquetball, their pleasant social evenings at the bar and he also alluded to some shared work interests in the investment field without elaborating further. There was a nervous shuffling of feet when he got to this part, and Claire and Tia both wondered what that was all about. They knew that John was making the rounds but thought that they'd better follow up as well.

Hilda didn't choose to speak and, although Gus had been asked, she also declined. Claire got up to make some final remarks about Marion, recalling what a kind, gentle soul she'd been, how concerned she always was

about Bill and how happy she'd been for the way things
had finally worked out for him. Bill surprised
everybody by suddenly standing up at that point,
tipping over his chair in the process. He turned to face
the people in the room and said, "Marion good to me.
She always there. I miss…" and with that he sat down.
Claire sat down too.

Jimmy got up and said, "If anyone wishes to have a
moment with the cremains, they are here and with that
he pulled back a curtain that had been concealing them.
There was a moment of silence in the room followed by
a few gasps of surprise. Hilda had not said anything
publicly for, about, or against either of the deceased but
her choice of urns spoke volumes. On the left side was
a bust of a smiling Marion welded to a heavy metal
book-like base that held her ashes. On the right side,
was a small, unmarked cedar box that held Gary's
ashes. After a further pause, Jimmy spoke again.
"Please feel free to mingle now. The buffet will be out
in about 20 minutes."

Claire and Tia looked at each other in shock, but
they both realized there was no time to process this
anomaly now. After sizing up the people in the room,
Claire said, "I'll take Dave if you'll take Janet, the
receptionist, Tia."

"Fine with me. Let's go."

Claire's conversation with Dave Stout was
disappointing. He gave away very little, basically
reiterating what he'd already said in his public remarks.
Tia had better luck with the receptionist. Tia asked
Janet what it had been like to work with Gary and was
basically told that he wasn't the nice guy everybody
thought he was.

"What do you mean?" Tia asked in as sympathetic a
tone as she could muster.

"He was a user and a snob. He never had a pleasant word for me or even noticed if I was alive unless he wanted something. Then he could suddenly get all oily. He was always on the lookout for rich clients. I guess they all are but he was just more aggressive about it. If I assigned a particularly plummy client to somebody else, he'd demand to know why I hadn't sent the person his way."

"Well, he didn't seem like that when I saw him at home with Hilda and Marion!" Tia replied, placing a shocked look on her face.

"Ah, Marion. He hated her," Janet said bluntly. "'She's messing up my life style,' I overheard him say on numerous occasions. And I also *accidentally* picked up the phone a few times when his wife called and those conversations were not pleasant. He'd start by asking her for something, sometimes money, and when she said no, he'd get all nasty."

"Why would he need money from her?" Tia asked, a carefully planted note of doubt in her voice. "Surely he made good money?"

"Yes, but he spent it, too."

"On what? Their house is pleasant enough but nothing special. His car was pretty sharp but not exactly a Mercedes!"

"I don't know. All I know is he was always nervous and always implied he was short of cash—leaching coffee off people—and cigarettes."

"Cigarettes! I didn't know he smoked? I never saw him smoke at home."

"No, and I'm sure his wife didn't know either. He was always pretty furtive about it."

"Do you suppose he had a girlfriend?" Tia asked in a low voice. "That would suck up the money!"

"Not that I know of. He flirted around the office a little bit but it always seemed half-hearted. Sometimes I wondered if he was even interested in women."

"I wouldn't know anything about that," Tia said. "Well, I guess I should move on. It's been nice talking with you." People were starting to look in their direction as their conversation had been rather prolonged and Tia decided she'd better wrap it up.

Chapter 48: Homing in on the Next Target.

When Matthew and Amanda arrived home from the memorial service, he turned to her and said, "That was him at the service!"

"Who?"

"Dave Stout, that friend of Gary. He was one of the men I saw at the gym that day."

"Was he the one who chased after you, or after the bus?"

"I don't know for sure. It could have been but I can't remember that part very well. I was scared and I was just concentrating on getting away."

"We'll have to tell Sergeant Crombie."

"But what can he do?"

"I don't know. But at least he should be able to bring him in for questioning. Somebody did break into your locker!"

"But there's no proof it was him just because he was there that day."

"I'll talk to Tia and Claire about it. Tia could talk to the sergeant. He at least listens to her."

"I thought he listened to you, too?"

"Yes, sometimes, but I think it's more because I'm an old lady and he listens out of respect. Tia, I think, he takes more seriously."

"I guess I screwed up. Maybe I should have talked to him myself at the service. Got him to admit that he'd been there. Mentioned that my locker had been broken into."

"No!" Amanda said. "It's good that you didn't. We don't want him knowing where you live or anything about you, including that you know the rest of us. He could be connected with that motorcycle bunch, for all we know."

Both of them went to bed that night feeling frustrated and unsettled. It wasn't clear if they were any further ahead or not in their investigation or where they should go next.

The next morning, Matthew went to school and Amanda went next door to see Tia as soon as she saw Jimmy leave for work. It was a beautiful, mild, February day with a false promise of spring in the air and Amanda could have been almost happy if this situation was not weighing on her so heavily.

Tia was shocked and excited to hear what Matthew had discovered and she immediately picked up the phone and called Sergeant Crombie. He wasn't available but she left a message for him to call her back urgently. Then she got Amanda some coffee and warmed up a piece of apple cake for her.

"How do you do that?" Amanda asked. "Bake the cake with the apple slices on top without having them dry out?"

"You melt jelly and spoon it over them beforehand."

"Umm," Amanda replied tersely. "Tasty." She kept the rest of her thoughts to herself.

The phone rang then and it was Sergeant Crombie calling. "Hello, Michael," Tia responded, and Amanda raised her eyebrows. Tia told him what they knew and then mentioned that Amanda was with her and could better fill him in on the whole scenario that had happened to Matthew at the gym. She put the phone on speaker and Amanda explained.

"I'm going to share this with McCoy," the sergeant responded. "He's pretty frustrated himself about the lack of progress in finding out who was behind that car crash and whether or not it was linked to the motorcycle gang or was just a one-off with that Fil Deijers."

"But what can he do?"

"Well, for one thing we could ask this Dave Stout to come in as a witness, explaining that Matthew had recognized him. We could ask him if he knew the other two men who were at the gym that day. We could tell him that Matthew found the memory stick which he subsequently shared with us and that we're pretty sure that was what the thief was after when he broke into his locker."

"I never thought of approaching him as a witness," Amanda broke in admiringly. "Clever!"

"We can also ask a judge for a subpoena saying we now have a pretty good idea that the sixth file was generated in Gary's office. Between that and the locker break-in in Dave Stout's presence, the judge might consider that enough evidence to warrant a search of Stout's files."

"It never happens that easily on TV," Amanda warned, thereby losing in one stroke whatever progress she'd made in her relationship with Sergeant Crombie.

"Well, we'll see," Sergeant Crombie said. "Please ask Matthew to call me so we can arrange a time for him to come in. Then we'll take it from there. Thanks for letting us know." And with that he hung up the phone. Tia just looked at Amanda and shook her head.

Chapter 49: Finally, Some Progress—Maybe

Dave Stout was duly brought into the station and from behind a one-way mirror, Matthew confirmed the identification. He was asked if he recalled the day a young man's locker had been broken into. At first, Stout denied it, but then pretended to recall it.

"A memory stick was found in Gary Boaz' locker that day by this same enterprising young man. He kept it with him in his pocket so it was not in the locker at the time it was broken into. He subsequently turned it over to us and we found the contents to be very interesting!" McCoy looked carefully at Stout when he said this. He definitely looked uncomfortable. "According to his wife, Hilda, you knew Gary very well. Would you know anything about that memory stick?"

Stout shook his head. "No. We didn't talk much about business when we were out together. We were either playing ball, talking about sports or just generally chewing the fat."

"I see," McCoy said. "Well, our forensic analysis has revealed that one of the files on that memory stick was not prepared by Gary and we'd like to find out where it came from. Did you ever share a file with him?" Michael Crombie raised his eyebrows slightly when he heard the term *forensic analysis*, but he recognized its use as one of McCoy's intimidation tactics.

"No-o," Stout stuttered. "Why would I?"

"Gary was apparently doing some work on off-shore investments of a not entirely legal nature. Were you aware of that?" Stout just shook his head. "Please answer out loud for the record. This interview is being taped," McCoy admonished.

"No."

"Are you involved in any work with members of a motorcycle club?"

Stout did not respond immediately but then said, "I can't answer that for reasons of confidentiality."

"I se-e-e," McCoy said meaningfully. Stout shifted uncomfortably in his chair.

"There was a break-in in Gary's office after his death. Do you know anything about that?"

"No."

"There was also a break-in in his house and an attempt made to steal his computer just before the office break-in. Were you aware of that?"

"No."

It was clear that they were not going to get any more information out of Dave Stout that day so McCoy brought the interview to an end and Sergeant Crombie led him out of the office and thanked him for his time. They watched him walk away and both recognized that he was looking quite shaken.

"Do you think we could get a subpoena to search his files?" Crombie asked.

"I doubt it," McCoy responded. "I wonder if the girls can do anything?" By *the girls*, McCoy was referring to Tia, Claire, Gus and Amanda. He'd come so far as to recognize that they had rendered and could continue to render some useful assistance to him and Crombie in certain of their investigations. However, he was not yet ready to grant them any greater status than that of well-meaning amateurs who bumbled along and occasionally and, quite accidentally, uncovered some answers.

Sergeant Crombie faithfully reported the rather unsatisfying results of Dave Stout's interrogation to Tia who then passed them on to the rest of the group. It was Thursday by this time and the group met that evening to discuss where to go next.

"I think we have to bring Sean in on this," John commented. "Between the two of us, perhaps we can find a way to access Dave's files."

"What about the receptionist?" Tia asked. "Would she help? She certainly didn't have a very high opinion of Gary. Maybe she feels the same about Dave."

"We don't know if we can trust her," Amanda objected.

"I can ask Sean what he thinks. He's had more dealings with her than I have," John offered.

Nobody else had any other ideas and the meeting ended shortly thereafter. It was definitely one of their less productive and less satisfying get-togethers.

Chapter 50: A Baby and a Break-through

Claire's phone rang at five the next morning. It was Jimmy calling. "Claire, I thought you'd want to know. Tia's at the hospital. The baby's coming but she's having some trouble." Jimmy's voice was shaking and despite the underlying ripples of enmity between them, Claire knew he was calling her for help.

"I'm on my way, Jimmy. University Hospital, right?"

"Yes. Fifth floor. Maternity Ward. I'm in the parent's room. I'll tell them to let you in."

"See you in twenty minutes or so, Jimmy! Hang in there." Claire hung up the phone and told Dan what had happened as she hurriedly dressed. The call had woken him up.

"I'll get Jessie off to school and who should I call to cover for you with Roscoe?"

Claire thanked him, gave him the information, hurriedly finished dressing and raced out the door.

When she entered the waiting room outside the surgery, she found Jimmy sitting in a corner with his head in his hands. "The baby's in distress and they have to do an emergency C-section!" he said without formally greeting her. "But her blood pressure shot way up and they have to get it under control before they can go ahead!"

"My understanding is that they can administer a drug that almost instantly lowers the blood pressure," Claire said soothingly. "It should be okay, especially since they're not going to allow her to proceed with a natural delivery."

"But what if it's not? What if she dies or if the baby is like…" Jimmy stopped at that point, realizing what he'd just said. But Claire just smiled.

"Don't worry, Jimmy. The chances of having a baby as damaged as Jessie are exceedingly rare. But how did all this happen? Why does she need a C-section?"

The doctor says she has a full-on case of Placenta Praevia and he was very angry that the technicians and other professionals involved hadn't caught it earlier!"

"How long has Tia been in there?"

Just then, the door to the operating room opened and the surgeon came out to talk to Jimmy. He was holding a small bundle in his arms and approached Jimmy with a smile. Jimmy stood up and the surgeon handed him his baby daughter. Jimmy just gawked at her, too upset to really take it in. "Tia?" was all he could manage.

"She's in the recovery room and a nurse is with her. She's being monitored closely. We'll keep her in for a couple of days. We're still trying to find out why her blood pressure spiked so dangerously but it's under control now."

"Can I see her?" Jimmy asked. "I need to see her."

"Just for a minute but then she has to rest." The two of them, with Jimmy holding the baby tightly, walked off together.

Claire was struggling hard with her own emotions. She wanted very much to see Tia for herself so she could know if she was really all right or not, and she wanted to see the baby. So far, Jimmy hadn't even given her a peek. In fact, he seemed to have forgotten that Claire was even there. She sat down to wait for Jimmy's return, recognizing once again that since he'd come into Tia's life, Claire's place in it had dropped considerably.

"She's doing okay, Claire. I told her you were here," Jimmy said, when he returned. "I'm going to stay here but you don't need to."

"I'm going over to your house to let Mario know and make sure he gets off to school okay."

"Thanks!" Jimmy said gratefully.

But Claire did not leave immediately. Since she'd come this far, she thought she'd go up to the unit where Mike Miller was and check on his progress. It was still only 6:30 in the morning, so they certainly wouldn't let her see him but she could at least find out if he was in the same room.

When Claire arrived at the desk in the unit, the clerk looked at her suspiciously. She explained why she was there so early and then asked about his progress.

"Are you a relative?" the clerk asked.

Claire braced herself before responding. "No, but I'm a close friend—and I have some very important news for him if he's able to hear it."

"He's awake but not very responsive," the clerk explained. "I doubt he'd be able to understand it. In any case, visiting hours are not until one this afternoon."

"Could you at least tell me what room he's in so when I come back I can go there directly?"

"Number 3, down this hall."

"Okay, thanks," Claire said, and turned away preparatory to leaving.

"And you're not to bring him any food," the clerk called after her.

Claire left the unit and sat down in the small waiting room near-by. Periodically she peeked through the window to see if the clerk was still at her desk. Ten minutes later, she saw that the desk was empty and quickly entered the unit and slipped into room number 3. Fortunately, Mike was the only one in it.

He was awake and when she approached his bed, she said "Do you remember me, Mike?"

He looked at her dazedly, but finally nodded his head slightly.

"How are you?" Mike gave her a blank stare.

"Do you remember what you asked me to get my Aunt Gus to do for you in Barbados?"

Again there was the blank stare. Finally, he nodded his head slightly.

Claire told him quickly that they'd succeeded and that she had the papers at home to prove it. "I didn't bring them because I was visiting a friend who just had a baby." Mike just looked at her.

"You promised to tell me something if I did this for you, remember?"

Mike continued to regard her with a dazed expression on his face. His eyes kept closing momentarily as if he were drifting off to sleep. Finally, he seemed to rouse himself a little and muttered, 'Gary, h...'".

"Yes, I want to know who arranged to kill Gary. You..."

"What are you doing in here?" asked an outraged nurse who'd just popped in the door. "I'm going to call security."

Claire brushed by her and hurriedly left, taking the stairs. Fortunately, Mike was only on the third floor so she was able to exit the building quickly.

Chapter 51: When in Doubt, Ask the Husband

Claire left, feeling both frightened and ridiculous. Why did she always get herself into these situations? What had Mike been about to say? Did he even know what he was saying? Dave must be involved in this somehow but how were they going to find out?

It was 8:30 when she finally got home after telling Mario about his baby sister, reassuring him that his mother was okay and that he could see her later that afternoon, and getting him off to school. Dan met her at the door. "The bus left with Jessie ten minutes ago," he said, "and I was just leaving for the office. How's Tia doing? Has the baby come yet?"

Claire didn't respond directly. "I need to talk to you, Dan? Do you really have to go in this morning?"

"No-o," he said slowly. "I suppose I could go in this afternoon. I don't have a meeting or an appointment. I just wanted to catch up on some work I need to do there. Is it important?"

"Yes. I need you," Claire said simply. Dan put his arms around her then. "I need you, too," he said humorously, "but you never seem to be around when my need is the greatest."

"Not in that way!" she said, annoyed, and shook his arms off. "I need you to be my friend and just listen to me!"

Dan took a step back and just looked at her. "Okay," he said softly. "Let's just sit down at the table. I could use a second cup of coffee. What about you? Have you had any breakfast?"

Claire shook her head. "No, I'm not hungry yet. I just need to talk. Let's get our coffee and sit in the living room. I need to run some things by you and get your opinion."

Once they were comfortably seated, Claire began. First, she told him all that she knew about Tia and the baby. "I just saw the baby for a second. She looks all right."

"Let's just hope," Dan said grimly. "I wouldn't want Tia and Jimmy to go through what we've gone through."

Claire told him then all about what had been happening with Gary's computer and the various leads they'd been tracking down. Finally, she confessed her surreptitious meeting with Mike in his hospital room that morning and Dan just shook his head. "All Mike said before we were interrupted was, 'Gary—h...' and I don't know what that means. Dave must be involved somehow but there doesn't seem to be any way to get to his records."

"What about the income tax people?" Dan asked. "Has McCoy thought of that?"

No-o-o, I don't think he has," Claire said slowly. "I'll phone him this morning and ask."

"You'll phone him? I thought the two of you couldn't stand each other. Isn't Tia the one who usually calls him when it's necessary?"

"Donald McCoy and I have a peculiar relationship—but it's a relationship. I think he's come to respect me in a certain way. He'll want to hear this idea. According to what Sergeant Crombie told Amanda, he's really feeling frustrated about the whole situation."

They talked a bit more but it was clear that Claire was feeling better since she had a new lead to follow up. Dan was now the one who seemed to be on edge and he convinced Claire that she'd feel better still if she went back to bed for a while and even better if he were to keep her company. She complied but grabbed a notepad and pencil on the way and scribbled a short to-do list to herself before settling back under the covers.

Later that morning when Dan had gone off to work, Claire made the call to McCoy. He admitted to her, as Amanda had said, that he was feeling very frustrated about this case. She confessed to him that their little group had had a chance to go over the contents of the sixth file while not exactly admitting that they'd made a copy. "It read like a double ledger and seemed like a pretty clear indication of money laundering. Isn't that something the tax people would be interested in? Couldn't they get a subpoena?"

There was silence for a minute and then McCoy replied. "It's worth a try," he said. "I'll call them. Thanks," he added grudgingly.

"One other thing," Claire said hastily before he could hang up the phone. "I heard Hilda say once that Gary was carrying a lot of junk in his car. Were the forensic people able to figure out what it was?"

"Why do you ask?"

"Oh, just thinking."

He didn't ask her what, but he also didn't shut her down like he would've done in the past. He knew better now. "I'll check over the forensic report again and get back to you," he said.

Chapter 52: Claire's Motto: When You Can't Act, Think

After talking to Inspector McCoy, Claire checked her watch. It was 11:45, still two hours to wait before visiting hours at the hospital. And Claire was afraid to go back to Mike's room anyway in case she ran into the same nurse. She made some lunch and then did some laundry. She thought about dinner but decided to suggest to Dan that they go out that evening since they had help for Jessie until ten.

At exactly two o'clock, Claire arrived at the maternity ward at the University Hospital to visit Tia. Claire was shocked to see how weak Tia looked and hugged her gently. Tia's parents had been there earlier but had gone out for a break and Jimmy had left so he could bring Mario to meet the baby when he arrived home from school. Thus Claire and Tia had a special hour alone together to share the happiness of the baby's safe arrival.

Tia rang and asked that the baby be brought in so Claire could see her. Claire examined her closely, wanting to satisfy herself that the baby was okay. Tia watched her anxiously, waiting to hear what she had to say. "I don't see any problem," Claire said finally, and she placed the baby gently beside Tia. They talked about Tia's future plans for fitting the baby into her life, about how her arrival might affect Mario, about how happy Jimmy was. In fact, they talked about everything except the case. There were things going through Claire's head, though. Things she wanted to check out.

After visiting Tia, Claire did manage to make it to Mike's room upstairs without being noticed and peeped in the door. But she could see he was in a deep sleep and left silently. When she got home, she phoned Inspector McCoy back. He informed her that the tax people had been very interested and were arranging for a warrant. He gave her the information she'd requested earlier and then asked her why she wanted it, but Claire did not reply directly. She only said that she'd be back to him immediately if she found out anything of value about the case.

At four that afternoon, Dan phoned to say he'd be working late and probably wouldn't get home before 6:30. Claire suggested they meet at Sorrentino's Restaurant on Calgary Trail instead and eat dinner there and Dan agreed.

"How was your day?" he asked when he joined her there at a quiet booth in the corner.

"It was fine," she replied, and they spent most of their evening talking about Tia's baby and what they could do to help out. "Her mother will be staying for a couple of weeks so she'll do the cooking and help with caring for the baby. And Jimmy is taking a week off so she'll have plenty of help right now." They talked then about what Claire could do to help her once the extra supports were gone.

"Did you ever find out what happened to her during delivery?" Dan asked.

"No. The doctors still haven't been able to explain it."

Claire was quiet then and Dan thought about asking her about the case since she hadn't volunteered any information. But he saw a look in her eye, a kind of hooded look that he recognized when she was thinking about something but didn't want to share. He left it alone.

They talked about Jessie then and Claire became more animated. "I think we can say at this point that she has made the adjustment to her new school and is beginning to thrive there." The school board had arbitrarily transferred, Jessie, age 13, to a junior-senior high school at the beginning of that school year and the early months had proven to be a very tough transition for her. But now, three quarters of the way through the academic year, she finally seemed to be settling in. "Jessie certainly enjoys her drama class and Bertha appears to have done all right with her during Aunt Gus's absence. I talked to the teacher, Brian Littner, and he feels Bertha is actually enjoying it!"

"But how does Gus feel about that? Isn't she going to take over again?"

"She has mixed feelings. She says that she has really enjoyed being there with Jessie and feels very close to her. But she feels that Jessie needs to strengthen her relationship with Bertha who has overall responsibility at school for her by sharing some of the fun times. Still, Aunt Gus seemed very sad when she said it."

"Do you think our Jessie has actually been able to socialize Gus when nobody else could?" Dan asked humorously but with an edge of pride and wonder.

"I think Jessie has brought out the good in a lot of people," Claire said softly. *Including me,* she added to herself.

Soon after, the evening came to an end and they went home feeling happy and relaxed. At least, Dan felt relaxed. Claire felt fine except for the sense of having a coiled snake in her chest, but this sensation she didn't share with Dan.

Chapter 53: Time for Action

Claire was at the restaurant with Roscoe and Bill the next morning, overseeing their work placements there, when her phone rang. She was surprised to hear Inspector McCoy's voice. He was not usually so prompt about getting back to her. "You were right about that file being funny, Claire," he said in an unusually gleeful tone. The Feds got the warrant yesterday afternoon. They went right to the office and confiscated all of Stout's files and worked on them late last night. Then they applied for further warrants this morning for the pizzeria and the two motorcycle clubs, and expect to uncover a bonanza! From what they know already, both Dave Stout and Gary Boaz were laundering and sheltering money for a number of people in both the Hell's Angels and Rebel Kings motorcycle clubs. The Hells insisted that both Gary and Dave invest in the pizzeria chain they set up so that they'd be implicated and couldn't sell them out. You mentioned a while ago—or maybe it was Tia—that Gary always seemed short of money so maybe that was the reason."

"But did you find any connection to Gary's murder?"

"No-o," McCoy admitted.

"I thought so," Claire said.

"What do you mean?"

"Nothing," Claire replied. "I'll be in touch if I learn anything. Thanks!"

After the phone call, Claire mulled over the situation while she helped Bill to trim and slice Bok Choy for the Japanese beef and vegetable lunch special of the day. But as she worked, she continued to think. When Bill went off for his afternoon coffee break, Claire made a phone call to Hilda to arrange a visit and then went to see how Roscoe was doing at the checkout. He'd improved remarkably in the past few months and now rarely made a mistake. When orders became too complicated for him to calculate easily, he called on one of the servers who sometimes functioned as cashier for assistance but this was happening less and less. The books continued to balance and it looked like he was doing a reliable job—a job in which he took great pleasure and satisfaction.

After her shift ended at four, Claire went home to check on Jessie. Her after school assistant was there but Claire asked her to do some cleaning and organizing tasks that always needed catching up on so Jessie and she could have some mother-daughter time together. Claire then wheeled Jessie into the den and closed the door.

"Jessie, I have to talk to you," she said simply. Jessie tilted her head in Claire's direction and waited patiently. Claire told her the story then, or at least the highlights of all that had been happening. She ended by telling her about Mike in the hospital, what had happened and what he'd said. And then her voice cracked.

Jessie looked at her then, almost as if she could see, although the specialists had long ago determined that she was functionally blind. 'Cortically blind' they called it. Her face changed suddenly. It got that look she had when she was trying to communicate—and at that moment Claire knew. "Thanks, Jessie. I understand," she whispered. Then Claire wheeled her into the living room and informed the assistant that she was going out for a while.

When Hilda answered the door, she saw a look of grim purpose on Claire's face and many times during the next hour, Job, had occasion to growl at her. But Claire continued single-mindedly with her grilling, trying to extract every ounce of information about Gary she could from Hilda.

When Claire left, she looked calmer and more satisfied than she had when she'd arrived. Hilda was crying softly, but there was not anything Claire could do about that. She hadn't caused this terrible situation. Again she had little to say to Dan that evening and nothing at all about the case. And again, he knew better than to ask.

The next morning, Claire called Inspector McCoy again. He sounded faintly irritable on the phone. "I'm meeting with the tax inspectors in half an hour to go over their findings. Do you have any new information? If not, I'll talk to you later."

"Yes, I think so. Can you arrange another interview with Dave Stout or do the Feds consider him their property now?"

"Why? What do I have left to talk to him about?"

"Ask him how he arranged Gary's murder. Tell him you know that he did it. Be your most bullying and intimidating self. Get him to crack. I think you'll find what he has to tell you very interesting."

"And what will that be?"

"I'm not saying but I think you'll be very surprised."

"Well, I don't see how I can do that. I don't have the evidence to make a charge like that."

"Tell him nobody else knew the exact time Gary was going to the airport. You did say there was a call from him to Gary on the phone about that time. You don't have to mention the second call. We've explored every other avenue. Tell him that and tell him he's the only viable suspect."

"That's pretty thin," McCoy argued. "I don't think I can do that."

"Can't or won't? Just tell him what Hilda said, that from the way Gary had been acting before his death it was apparent that something was bothering him. Maybe he was scared of the rough group he was hanging around with. Maybe he was planning to come clean about the tax evasion schemes. In that case, he would have dragged Dave down with him. Dave must have known that. It's more than enough motive for murder!"

McCoy took a long time to respond and when he did, he talked slowly despite his pending appointment. "I'm at a dead end on this case. I guess I don't have much to lose by giving it a try. I'll get him in tomorrow."

"If you learn anything and plan to call Hilda with the results, let me know in advance so I can be there with her when you visit, please."

Again McCoy hesitated but then he agreed.

Chapter 54: Finally, an Answer!

Claire was just getting ready for work the next morning when the phone rang. It was Inspector McCoy. "Sergeant Crombie and I plan to visit Hilda at about ten this morning. You asked me to let you know if we were planning to contact her."

"What? ..." Claire asked. But McCoy cut her off.

"I have to go. We'll see you later," he replied, and the line went dead.

Claire hastily made arrangements for yet another substitute to work with poor Roscoe, hoping that the events of the day would mean that this would be his last for a while. Then she called Hilda to ask if she could come over and was very glad that she did.

"Oh, I was just on my way out the door," Hilda said grudgingly. "I need more dog food. We're all out."

Claire found it a little eerie the way Hilda talked about Job as if he were another person but tried to understand how traumatized Hilda had been. "I'd be happy to pick it up for you. How much do you want and where should I buy it?" Claire asked.

Hilda was relieved to unload this responsibility on Claire and gave her directions. It was a bit of a drive and Claire hastened to get ready, not wanting to be late for the arrival of the police. Traffic was slow and then made slower by a fender bender reducing cars to one lane. By the time she'd gone all the way south to Ellerslie Road and back, a full hour had passed and she cruised into Hilda's driveway at two minutes to ten, feeling nervous sweat drip down her back.

Hilda opened the door and looked surprised to see the tense expression on Claire's face. Claire hastily described the traffic troubles, exaggerating for effect in order to cover for her obviously wrought up state. They had just settled into the living room with coffee when the bell rang again.

"Who can that be?" Hilda asked, addressing Job, not Claire. Claire just shook her head. Hilda answered the door and stepped back in surprise.

"May we come in?" Inspector McCoy asked. "We have some further news about the case." She settled them in the living room and made a perfunctory offer of coffee, which they both refused. "We've been interviewing a new suspect in the death of your husband," McCoy began. "Dave Stout."

"Dave?" Hilda asked. "That doesn't make sense. They were thick as thieves."

"True that!" Sergeant Crombie interjected, taking the opportunity to practice some modern lingo he'd picked up from his young nephew.

McCoy glared at him and then said, "He was the only one besides you who knew that Gary would be driving your mother to the airport that morning. We picked that up from our first interview with him some time ago. Also it appears that he was involved with Gary in the money laundering and off-shore transfer of money from two different motorcycle clubs."

"Ugh," Hilda grunted with a pained look on her face. "What did he say?"

"He denied it—but he did say he knew how it happened."

Hilda waited for McCoy to say more and she saw the look that passed between him and Sergeant Crombie. She steeled herself.

"I'm sorry to tell you that the accident was the result of an elaborate plan on your late husband's part to get rid of your mother. He hired Fil Deijers to deliberately ram them on the front passenger door—and he and Fil arranged the accident spot in advance."

Hilda said nothing. Job, as usual, was beside her and he rubbed his face against her knee. She stroked his head absently. She looked at nobody. It was as if nobody else was in the room—except the dog. And then a look of peace came over her face. Another minute passed and then she said, "At least he got the death sentence for his crime—and so did his accomplice."

Sergeant Crombie and Inspector McCoy left a few minutes later, glad to be gone. Hilda still sat inertly and Claire remained frozen in her chair watching her. Finally, Hilda said, "It's a relief to know. But I think I knew already. That's why I've been feeling so hateful towards him since the accident. At least I don't have to feel guilty about that anymore—or for holding them up at the door when they left for the airport. Gary was obviously in phone contact with that man. That was probably the other call on his phone the police couldn't trace. So it wouldn't have mattered when they left. That Fil was waiting for them."

After this speech, Hilda sat silently and outwardly composed. Claire did not dare move nor did she respond. The minutes passed. Ten minutes later, Hilda got up quickly and ran to the bathroom. Retching sounds followed. Then she returned and crumpled back into her chair, her tears flowing freely and mingling with the taste of bile in her mouth. Finally, she was silent again and Claire crossed the floor and knelt beside her. "Would tea help at all?" she asked softly.

"Maybe," Hilda gasped—and Claire left to prepare it. But when she returned, Hilda just turned her head away and asked for water. Claire got her the water and then sat down again in her chair. Hilda had begun a strange, keening moan, rocking herself back and forth with her legs tucked under her. Finally, she said, "Talk to me about Marion." And Claire did, recalling all the kind, thoughtful things Marion had done in the time Claire had known her and stressing how unusual it was to be so un-judgmental as Marion was.

By this time another hour had passed and Claire was just thinking that she'd have to call Dan and ask him to get his own supper. The assistant would take care of Jessie and herself. But then she had an idea. Turning to Hilda she said, "Do you think that now we could have a proper wake for your mother with the people who remember her? The joint celebration you had was very nice but I never felt that it really captured Marion's spirit."

Hilda cried again and nodded her head. "Yes, no ... I mean—you're right, but I don't want anybody to know. It's too terrible. Maybe Jimmy and Tia—and Dan would be okay. But nobody else!"

"Look, maybe Tia can leave the baby with her mother for a few hours ... and I know Jessie will be okay with her assistant. I could ask Tia to bring something for supper and we could also order in. Why don't we just do it tonight, the five of us, just sit around and talk about Marion for a few hours? Would that work for you, Hilda?"

Hilda just looked at her dumbly but finally she nodded her head. Claire got busy organizing, the others arrived within the hour and finally the real good-byes to Marion began. They all shared their memories of her and when it was Tia's turn, she described some of the caring moments she'd seen between Marion and Bill and how much she'd respected how Marion always saw the good in people. But what happened next went beyond mere words.

Jimmy spoke then, remembering all that Marion had done for him while his sister, Mavis, was in the Calgary institution with Marion's nephew, Bill. "I was so angry with my former wife for refusing to have Mavis moved to Edmonton, and so torn by guilt that I don't think I could have gotten through those awful years without Marion. It wasn't only what she did for Mavis and me, always keeping an eye on her and phoning me or telling me during my visits when anything was wrong. It was also just what she was like as a person. It soothed me a lot just talking to her, just knowing that there were people like her in the world, considering what I had to go home to."

Tia quietly took his hand after Jimmy's unusually frank outburst. She turned to Hilda and said, "Jimmy and I have discussed this at some length and we both feel the same way. We want to honor Marion's memory and keep her alive forever in our hearts. The best way we could think of to do that was to name our daughter after her. We filled out and submitted the birth certificate today. Our daughter's name is Marion Marisa, after your mother and mine."

Hilda looked at her stunned. But after a moment, she reached over and hugged Tia fiercely, embracing Jimmy as well. "Thank you!" was all she could manage in a croaky voice.

Chapter 55: Cleaning Up Loose Ends

The next morning, Claire called Hilda to check on her. She was able to convince her that Gus, John, Amanda and Matthew had a right to know what had really happened since they'd worked so hard on Hilda's behalf to find the answer. Along with Jimmy and Tia, they all met again that night at Amanda's house.

Hilda and Job were a little late and before they arrived, Claire took the opportunity to ask Tia and Jimmy a question that had been burning inside her.

"Aren't you afraid that the names Mario and Marion will get mixed up? How does Mario feel about that? It's kind of like stealing his identity which I thought would be the last thing you'd want to do under the circumstances!" Claire was alluding to the fact that it was less than a year since Jimmy had adopted Mario and now he must be wondering if a natural-born child between Tia and Jimmy would replace him in some way.

"We did think of that," Tia said soberly, and Jimmy nodded his head. "The thing is the names will always be pronounced differently and we will vigorously correct anybody who doesn't recognize or respect that. *Mario* is an Italian name with Italian vowel sounds. That is quite different from the English *Marion*."

"O-o-h. That's why you're always correcting me when I mention his name! I thought you were just being precious!" Dan interjected. The others laughed but just then they heard Hilda arriving and changed the subject.

Meanwhile, Mario and little Marion were home next door with their grandparents and Marisa was allowing Mario to give his sister the bottle of breast milk Tia had left for her. Tia hadn't wanted Mario to hold the baby, afraid that something might happen. But Marisa knew that he could handle it and that this was something he needed to do.

For Mario, as for Jimmy, Marion's birth was a form of completion. He felt even more now than before that he was part of a real family. So Claire need not have worried. The relationship between Mario and Jimmy was very solid and neither of them had any concerns or doubts about his place.

Next door, the meeting got underway with Claire in her usual, take-charge role. She began by getting a commitment from those not present the night before, as well as a recommitment from those who'd been present, that they would keep confidential what they were about to hear.

Tia spoke first because Inspector McCoy had phoned her when he couldn't reach Claire with some follow-up details. From the interview with Dave Stout, he'd learned that Dave was the one who'd attempted to steal Gary's computer from Hilda's house and had shot the dog. He was also the one who'd broken into Matthew's locker at the gym but he denied trying to follow him. The man running to board the bus was probably just a coincidence.

Dave also denied trashing Gary's office so Inspector McCoy sent Sergeant Crombie to the jail where the three Hell's Angels members were incarcerated to re-interview them. One of them, Ron, finally admitted that it was they who broke into Gary's office, fearing he had some incriminating evidence that would eventually be uncovered.

Hilda spoke next, recalling that Gary had started putting *junk* in his car a couple of weeks before the accident but it was a particular kind of junk. For example, he stored a thick, memory foam mattress in the back seat of his small sports car and it always ended up curling around the driver's door on the inside. He told Hilda that he wanted to keep it handy in case he ever needed to stay really late at work and needed a nap.

"Didn't you wonder what that was really about?" Matthew asked.

"It crossed my mind that he might be entertaining a woman in his office late at night—he often worked late—and needed a place to bed down. But I didn't really think he was the type and after that I never thought much about it. We hadn't been close for a long time."

"What else did he store in his car?" Gus asked.

"He also had a piece of ¾-inch plywood wedged between the front passenger seat and the driver's console and, as a result, the impact from the van drove my mother into the plywood rather than into Gary," Hilda replied in a strained voice.

John looked at her sympathetically and asked in a quiet voice, "How could he possibly explain that!"

"He said there was a leak in the passenger window and he always felt the draft on his legs. He said he was going to get it fixed and if the mechanic couldn't fix it then at least he could take the board out when the weather warmed up."

Hilda was looking quite queasy at this point and Tia said, "You don't need to tell us anymore. It's too horrible—and it must be very painful for you."

"No, I want to finish! It helps me to understand, to come to terms with it," Hilda replied and then went on. "I remember that he was wearing a heavy turtleneck that day and his neck looked unusually thick. But maybe it was my imagination."

"I don't think so," Claire said. "I asked McCoy to talk further to the pathologist about some of the unusual findings. There was some remaining flesh on Gary's neck and it looked like it had some specific burn marks on it. The forensic team also found unexplained bits of metal among the front seat springs. They could have come from a neck brace."

Hilda looked quizzical for a moment and then her mouth opened involuntarily in a classic *aha* gesture. "Gary played pick-up hockey during the winter with a few friends at our neighborhood rink—and he generally played goalie. I cleaned out his hockey bag the other day and I was wondering why I couldn't find his neck brace!"

An awkward silence followed, with the group members looking shocked and horrified. Claire jumped in to break the silence. "Is there anything else you can tell us, Hilda, or should I go on with my part?"

"No, that's it."

"Tell us how you knew, Claire—because clearly you did. Otherwise, you wouldn't have been able to tell McCoy what to do with Dave," Tia demanded.

"It started with what Mike said in the hospital that day that your baby was born, Tia. He only said one word—Gary—and then a sound like an *h*. I thought he didn't say more because the nurse interrupted us. But a couple of days later, I was talking to Jessie and telling her the whole story. She got that look on her face like she gets when she's really trying to tell me something––but of course she can't—because she can't talk. And that's when I knew. Mike also had that look, that look like he wasn't sure he would be able to tell me so he had to get the most important words out first. So he did tell me. It was *Gary*—or maybe—*Gary, he*."

"Well, you can ask Mike now," Tia pointed out. "You said he was just coming out of the coma and that was several days ago, the day Marion was born, so he should be clearer in his head now. Is he still in the hospital?"

Claire shook her head sadly. "I haven't had a chance to tell any of you yet. I called his mother this afternoon to see if I could meet with him. He passed away yesterday morning. His internal injuries were just too severe!"

There were various gasps in response to this statement and Hilda said bitterly, "Another life ruined by Gary."

"Yes and no, Hilda," Claire commented. "There are two kind of people in those clubs. There are people like Mike who are just fascinated by motorcycles and the idea of being part of a club that's like a kind of brotherhood. And then there are others who basically use it as a cover for criminal activities. Mike's misfortune was that he put some of those others in touch with his cousin, Gary, and acted as a lookout for one of their robberies. He therefore knew more about them and their activities than they could be comfortable with. And when they heard he was planning to leave, they saw him as a loose end, a threat to them."

"How did they find that out anyway?" Gus asked. "You said you never told anyone."

"And who would I even tell?" Claire asked in irritation. "Anyway, his mother was determined to track down the source. There was this girl Mike liked and she was one of the young women hanging around the club. Mike's mother found her number in his room and called her. Apparently, Mike had told her about his plans, hoping that she might leave the club and move with him to Saskatoon when he started university. She was trying to figure out what to do and shared the story with a friend who just happened to be the girlfriend of Jerry Nickerson. And that friend told him. He was one of the three involved in the beat down."

"So really, all that money laundering and tax evasion and what happened to Mike had nothing to do with Marion's death?" Matthew queried.

"That's right," Claire said. "But we did bring some criminals to justice and that wouldn't have happened otherwise. Marion would be pleased about that!"

"Yes, she would," Hilda said softly. "She always thought of others first."

The End

ABOUT THE AUTHOR

 In her private life, Emma and her husband, Joe Pivato, have raised three children—the youngest, Alexis, having multiple challenges. Their efforts to organize the best possible life for her have provided some of the background context for this book and others in the Claire Burke series. The society that the Pivatos have formed to support Alexis in her adult years is described at http://www.homewithinahome.com/Main.html.

Emma's other cozy mysteries in the Claire Burke series are entitled *Blind Sight Solution, The Crooked Knife, Roscoe's Revenge,* and *Jessie Knows.*

65641576R00140

Made in the USA
Charleston, SC
04 January 2017